PUFFIN BOOKS

Love, Aubrey

'Quite simply the best book for girls of nine and over
that I have read for years' – *Independent*

'A wonderfully moving and sensitive story in which the redemptive
power of love restores one's faith in life' – *Daily Mail*

'A very special debut novel . . . a delicately wrought exposition
of grief and healing' – *Sunday Telegraph*

'Honest . . . brave' – *Financial Times*

'A bittersweet and heartbreaking story' – *Waterstones Books Quarterly*

'The simple, unmawkish power of LaFleur's writing to hold us close
to Aubrey whilst she mourns means that her emotional journey
quickly becomes ours too' – *Books for Keeps*

'A powerful and stunning debut that I'm still thinking about days
after finishing it' – Rebecca Colwell, Waterstones bookseller

'A powerful story about love, loss, and healing that goes far beyond
its targeted middle-grade audience' – reader, *amazon.com*

'The narrative voice that carries *Love, Aubrey* is so engaging and
honest that I read it all in one night' – *goodreads.com*

At a very young age, Suzanne LaFleur fell in love with stories. She loved stories so much that she decided that if she had to grow up, she would write new stories for kids to read. *Love, Aubrey* is her first book. Suzanne works with children in New York City and Boston.

suzannelafleur.com

Coming soon, also by Suzanne LaFleur

Eight Keys

Love, Aubrey

SUZANNE LaFLEUR

PUFFIN

PUFFIN BOOKS

Published by the Penguin Group
Penguin Books Ltd, 80 Strand, London WC2R ORL, England
Penguin Group (USA) Inc., 375 Hudson Street, New York, New York 10014, USA
Penguin Group (Canada), 90 Eglinton Avenue East, Suite 700, Toronto, Ontario, Canada M4P 2Y3
(a division of Pearson Penguin Canada Inc.)
Penguin Ireland, 25 St Stephen's Green, Dublin 2, Ireland (a division of Penguin Books Ltd)
Penguin Group (Australia), 250 Camberwell Road, Camberwell, Victoria 3124, Australia
(a division of Pearson Australia Group Pty Ltd)
Penguin Books India Pvt Ltd, 11 Community Centre, Panchsheel Park, New Delhi – 110 017, India
Penguin Group (NZ), 67 Apollo Drive, Rosedale, North Shore 0632, New Zealand
(a division of Pearson New Zealand Ltd)
Penguin Books (South Africa) (Pty) Ltd, 24 Sturdee Avenue, Rosebank,
Johannesburg 2196, South Africa

Penguin Books Ltd, Registered Offices: 80 Strand, London WC2R ORL, England

puffinbooks.com

First published in the USA by Wendy Lamb Books, a member of Random House, Inc. 2009
First published in Great Britain in Puffin Books 2009
Published in this edition 2010

3

Text copyright © Suzanne LaFleur, 2009

The moral right of the author has been asserted

Set in Goudy
Made and printed in Great Britain by Clays Ltd, St Ives plc

British Library Cataloguing in Publication Data
A CIP catalogue record for this book is available from the British Library

ISBN: 978-0-141-33474-5

www.greenpenguin.co.uk

Penguin Books is committed to a sustainable future
for our business, our readers and our planet.
The book in your hands is made from paper
certified by the Forest Stewardship Council.

For Jessica,
because I promised

Virginia

It was fun at first, playing house.

I made all my own meals. Crackers and cheese, three times a day.

I watched whatever I wanted on TV, all day.

It'd been a good three days: crackers and cheese for breakfast, TV; crackers and cheese for lunch, TV; crackers and cheese for dinner, TV, bed. Nothing to think about but TV and cheese. A perfect world.

Then I ran out of cheese.

There wasn't anything left in the freezer. The veggie drawer in the fridge had drippy brown lettuce and stinky carrots. A container of milk sat on the shelf. I opened it. It smelled awful too, so I put the cap back on and shoved it to the back of the fridge.

I checked my room for snacks. I peeked at the lower shelf of my nightstand, where I had set a plate with two chocolate-covered cookies for Jilly, the way Savannah always did. Jilly's cookies used to disappear, but I couldn't seem to get her to come round any more. Savannah probably ate the cookies herself. I picked one up and bit it, but it was hard stale.

I had to go shopping. I needed a break from TV anyway. I got some money from my sock drawer, taking just two of the twenty-dollar bills left over from my birthday. It was so long ago, my birthday. On the day I turned eleven, I didn't think I would be using the money in Gram's card to buy my own groceries.

Everything was different now.

I didn't want anyone at the store to notice me, so I put on a hat and sunglasses, like a movie star walking around a city.

I put my backpack on and set out for the grocery store. It was nice to be outside for a change. The summer air felt really hot, though, and soon there was sweat under my hat and running down my face behind the glasses. The disguise wasn't as glamorous as it had seemed.

I was excited to pick out anything I wanted at the store. I went to the aisle with the SpaghettiOs and lifted my sunglasses to examine the cans. I wanted the ones with meatballs. *Savannah likes the plain ones.* No, she liked – Savannah had liked the plain ones –

I suddenly felt very sick, there in the canned-goods aisle.

But I needed food. I put five cans of SpaghettiOs with meatballs into my trolley.

Because I wanted to run a healthy household, I figured I needed some vegetables. I got two cans of corn and one of green beans. I picked out a box of Cheerios and a carton of milk, a loaf of bread, packs of sliced turkey and ham and a bag of apples. I realized my backpack would feel heavy and figured that that was enough to eat, for a few days anyway.

I paid and made it out of the store without anyone recognizing me. I stopped at a bench and zipped the paper grocery bag into my backpack. I adjusted my hat and sunglasses and started to walk home, but that's when I noticed the pet store next to the grocery.

I wasn't on a schedule or anything. I had time to go inside.

A bell jingled on the door as I opened it. The store had a heavy smell of animals and the sounds of many noisy birds chirping.

There were three puppies in glass cages. I pressed my hand to one of the windows and the baby dog jumped against it.

That would be fun, to have a dog.

I took the wad of leftover money out of my pocket and looked at it. The puppies cost hundreds of dollars each. Even the rest of the money in my birthday card wouldn't have been enough.

In the back of the store were tanks of fish. In front of the tanks were rows of individual little bowls, each with one colourful fish inside. The sign said BETTA FISH $3.99.

On the very end of the row of bowls was a blue fish with purple-edged fins. He was looking right at me and waving one of his fins.

I wiggled my finger back at him, and looked at the money in my hand again.

I carefully carried the bowl to the counter. The lady there saw me coming and slapped a container of food down.

'It's two dollars extra,' she said.

'That's fine, ma'am.' I watched as she moved my fish into a plastic bag, tied it and handed it to me.

'What's his name?' she asked.

'Sammy,' I said.

I held his bag carefully in my hand the whole way home.

I had everything I needed to run a household: a house, food and a new family. From now on it would just be me, Aubrey, and Sammy – the two of us, and no one else.

We'd had a fish before, a goldfish. I found her old bowl with blue pebbles under the kitchen sink. I hummed as I rinsed the pebbles without soap to keep Sammy's water suds free. I made the water a little warm and dumped Sammy into it with his old water. I set him on my dresser.

'Welcome home,' I told him.

Footsteps sounded on the porch. I froze and listened.

Mail pushed through the slot. The metal flap slammed shut and I jumped. I caught my breath and tiptoed to the door to look at the mail. It was starting to pile up. I hadn't touched it in four days. A lot of it was still addressed to Gordon Priestly. Dad. A kid's magazine came for Savannah. *Highlights*. I gave the mail a good kick and went back to the kitchen to make a sandwich.

The phone rang. It hadn't done that recently. I stared at it. Two rings. Three rings. On the fourth I grabbed it.

'Mom?'

'What's that, dear?'

'Hello?'

'Aubrey, honey, it's Abigail Marshall, from church.'

Oh. Church. Those stupid church ladies were always in our business. They called Mom all the time. We'd been to those social events they insisted we go to. At least, we went until I shoved my chocolate-ice-cream cone onto Pennie Layne's white dress when she kept asking me to play and wouldn't leave me alone when I said I didn't want to. And one of those church ladies kept leaving us a gross casserole on the front porch every week, even now, three months after the funeral. Last week it was eggplant. Eck.

'Is your mother there? I've been meaning to catch up with her, see how you two are doing. We haven't seen you two since the Fourth of July picnic.'

'No, she's gone out for a little, ma'am,' I said.

'Will you tell her I called? We're trying to organize a

bake sale, and thought she might like to be involved. She used to love our community projects. It might help.'

I didn't see how it would help. What in the world would help?

'Yes, ma'am,' I said.

'So you'll have her call me?' Mrs Marshall asked.

'Well, actually, we're going on vacation here in a few hours. She'll call you when we get back.' I had just come up with a perfect story, as there was no car parked outside any more.

'Oh, wonderful! It will be good for the two of you to get out of the house. Give a holler if y'all need anything now, you hear?'

'Will do, ma'am,' I said. 'Goodbye.'

I slammed the phone down. No more answering the phone; it was too risky. I fished a red Sharpie out of the kitchen junk drawer and wrote on a piece of paper, ON VACATION. I got tape and stuck it on the outside of the front door, and slammed that too. I knew the rules: I couldn't let anyone, *anyone*, know that I was alone. I'd seen it on TV. Kids found alone had to go to foster homes. I wasn't going to be one of those kids. I was staying right here.

Maybe the sign would also keep away unwanted casseroles.

The phone started ringing all the time. It rang and rang. I didn't have anything to say to anyone who would call on the phone. I didn't answer it.

Cheerios for breakfast, half a can of SpaghettiOs for lunch, half a can for dinner.

Sometimes I stopped actually watching the TV and just lay there on the couch, watching the cobwebs on the ceiling dance in the fan's breeze, thinking nothing.

I was glad my bedroom was downstairs, off the kitchen. It meant I didn't have to go upstairs, to see the bedrooms with the closed doors.

Savannah's room hadn't been changed at all, I knew. No one had even made her bed. It was still strewn with tangled blankets and stuffed animals. Dirty clothes filled her wicker hamper. Crayons and coloured paper lay scattered on her artwork table.

The door to Mom and Dad's room was shut too, but it had been used since the wreck. Mom had tried to sleep there. I knew she really slept on the couch downstairs most nights, if she slept at all.

I was very glad to have Sammy, who needed his food pellet every few days.

I blew across the surface of the water in his bowl, making ripples that made him wiggle his fins.

'Goodnight, Samkins,' I said. 'I have everything the way you like it. See. The lava lamp is on. The blinds are down. The ceiling stars will glow. And the music's all ready.'

I turned off the light and climbed into bed. Then I listened to the waltzes Dad had bought for me and watched

Sammy swimming, swimming, swimming in his bowl. It wasn't hard to sleep, listening to the circles of music and watching the circles in the water. My eyes got tired. I knew I wouldn't dream.

I was lying on the couch again, in the daytime. What day was it? I wasn't sure.

'Sammy! What do you wish, you lonely blue fish?' I called.

I listened.

'Me too. But I want mine with ice cream!'

Poor Sammy. I wondered if he missed all the other fish from the store. Probably not. It had seemed crowded. Betta fish like their own space.

Me too, Sammy.

At least it was summertime. No one to take my attendance in the morning. No stupid kids to stare at me all day, or to treat me funny. No one to care a thing about me, and I didn't have to care about anyone else, either. That felt good, the way crackers and cheese had felt good.

I was watching TV again and the doorbell rang. It rang and rang. I ignored it. But it didn't stop. The doorbell kept ringing.

Do not answer that, I told myself.

But the bell kept ringing.

I thought maybe I could go crazy. I could go crazy listening to that *ding-dong, ding-dong* over and over and over and over and –

My head told my feet to stop, but they were running from the couch. My arms reached for the door and flung it open.

And there was Gram, standing on the porch, her eyes red but fiercely determined.

'Gram,' I said. 'What are you doing here?'

'I came to check on my girls,' my grandmother said.

'Why?' I asked.

'I've been calling on the phone, and no one answered.'

'It's broken,' I lied.

'I was worried. I'd heard from you two every week, and then, nothing . . .'

'So you came all the way down here from Vermont? How?'

'On the train,' Gram answered. 'And in a taxi.'

I saw that Gram held a small travelling bag. She must have put just a couple of things in it. A few changes of clothes. Some pyjamas. A toothbrush . . . Gram hated travelling.

She opened her arms, and I fell into them. For the first time since I'd been on my own, I was crying.

We sat on the couch, Gram running her soft fingers over my scalp. Her fingers stayed away from the scar above my temple, which is a word I didn't even know until I had the makings of a scar there.

'Where's my Lissie?' she asked.

Lissie. My mother, her daughter. Where was she?

'Just out for a little. She'll be back before dinner,' I lied again. I hadn't known that living alone would make me a liar, but it did. I couldn't tell her the truth, no way.

'Gram, read to me?'

'Okay, darling, like when you were little? You always loved a story . . .' Gram didn't finish her thought, but I heard it finish in my head. She used to say that a lot, and the same words always came next: *Savannah, she wouldn't ever sit for a story . . .*

'Let me get my book.' I went to my room and got the book I was reading and brought it to Gram, whose soft voice made me want to sleep, forever. I curled against her, using her stomach as my pillow.

Sunset would be late, but the light began to change to golden orange as Gram read. The afternoon was ending. Dinnertime. The time Gram expected Mom to come home.

'Maybe we should go start some dinner,' she said, putting my bookmark back between the pages. 'That way, your mom won't have to worry about it when she gets in.'

'Right,' I said. I continued to lie on the couch, afraid that if I moved I was going to have to ask for a bucket to be sick in.

'Come help me. I've never been good in other people's kitchens,' Gram said. I got up slowly, carefully, and followed her into the kitchen. I was behind her when she saw my cans. The eight of them, some still full, some empty, sitting in a line on the counter. She must have known then. Maybe she wasn't ready to believe it. I'd had ages, but I didn't believe it, either. Her eyes wandered to my open bedroom door, then through it to the dirty underwear, jeans and T-shirts on the floor.

'Well, let's see what to fix.' She went to the fridge, where the only food besides mustard and relish was the packs of turkey and ham. She took out the meat, got the bread and made three sandwiches, on three plates. She opened the can of green beans, and heated the contents in the microwave in a glass bowl with a cover. She nodded to me to bring everything to the table as it was ready, and I did. I filled three glasses with water and set them out. When everything was on the table, we eyed the third place setting. For several long moments, I glanced at the digital clock on the stove: 7:20. 7:28. 7:33. 7:38. 7:42. Cold green beans.

'She's not coming, is she?' Gram asked.

I looked down at my plate, my throat tightening. 'No,' I whispered.

Gram sighed. 'Aubrey.'

Pause.

'Do you know where she went?' Gram sounded as if she still hoped Mom was just out doing errands.

I shook my head.

'How long has it been?'

I stared at my uneaten green beans, counting them: one, two, three, four, five . . . fifteen, sixteen . . .

'Aubrey.'

'A week.'

'A week! You've been by yourself for a week?'

The phone rang. Terrific. Gram watched me not answer it.

'The phone?' she asked.

'Not so much broken,' I answered.

'Not so much,' she repeated. Then she jumped out of her chair and hurried to the phone. 'Hello?' she said. She sounded desperate, panicky. 'Oh, no, thank you, I'm not interested in a music survey.' She hung the phone up again, and turned round slowly. She walked back to the table and sat back down. It looked like she was thinking and thinking and trying to pick something to say. Then she seemed to forget that she was trying to think of something to say, and covered her face with her hands. She put her head on the table. She stayed like that, shaking, for a long time.

'Please don't be mad,' I whispered.

'Aubrey, why why why why didn't you call me?'

I didn't know why. I hadn't even thought of calling her. I couldn't look at her. I felt the reason start in my toes and work its way up into my chest, and finally it creaked out of my mouth.

'Don't be mad at Mom, either. Please.'

'Aubrey . . .'

'She's had such a hard time.' I was crying again. I wished Gram hadn't come.

'I know, honey, I know.' Gram came to my side of the

table and put her arms round me, rocking me, pressing my head against her, covering my scar with her palm.

'Why did she leave me?'

'I don't know. No matter how much we love someone, or think we know them, we can never know what it is like to be inside them. I'm so sorry, so, so sorry. I thought the two of you were going to get better together.'

'She's not sick!' I shouted, pulling away. 'She's just sad! You don't know.'

Gram looked like I had slapped her. But her eyes met mine, and they weren't mad. They were melting. She pressed me to her again, so we weren't looking at each other any more. She held on so tightly.

2

I woke in the morning to Gram's voice in the kitchen.

'Yes . . . No . . . You haven't heard from her? Okay, please call us if you hear something. Thank you.'

I climbed out of bed and opened my door.

'Did you find her?' I asked.

'No, honey. None of your aunts or uncles have heard from her, or any of the friends listed here by the phone. I'll start calling her out-of-state friends. Someone must have heard from her. Where's her address book?'

'She keeps it in the drawer by the phone.'

I fixed myself a bowl of cereal. We were out of milk again, so I took the bowl of dry Cheerios to the table and started eating them one at a time.

Gram opened the drawer and rummaged through it.

'Could you help me?' she asked.

'It's small and green,' I said.

Gram looked again, then shut the drawer. 'I'm going to use the bathroom,' she said.

While she was gone, I stopped eating. Quiet as could be, I tiptoed to the drawer and pulled it open.

The small green book was gone.

I spent most of the day in my room with the door shut, sitting on my bed and drawing on a clipboard. I was wearing my Disney World visor Uncle David had sent me and having a great time all by myself.

Until Gram threw my door open. She started picking up clothes off the floor and tossing them into a laundry basket. 'Were you ever going to do laundry?' she asked.

'I don't know how to use the washing machine,' I answered.

'Your room is a pigsty,' she said. 'Why are there cookies on your nightstand? Are you trying to attract bugs?'

'Those are Jilly's,' I said.

'Whose?'

'Nobody's.' I turned to face the wall.

I heard Gram put down the laundry basket. She came and sat on the bed next to me, though we were facing different directions.

'When did you get a fish?' she asked.

'His name is Sammy,' I said. 'And he doesn't like strangers.'

Gram was quiet for several minutes. I got back to my

drawing, a castle, with a moat and a drawbridge and four tall towers.

'We need to talk, duckling.'

'I'm very busy right now,' I said.

'Aubrey . . .' Gram gently took the clipboard and pencil out of my hands. 'I need your help if we are going to find her. I know it might not be easy for you – but can you tell me anything about the time before she left that would help us figure out where she would go?'

I turned round, but I kept my head tipped low so that Gram couldn't see my face under the visor. 'Please?' she asked.

'She never said anything about leaving.'

'Nothing?'

'No. She just, I don't know, stopped noticing I was there.'

'What do you mean?'

'Well, sometimes she would get new groceries, or wash and vacuum all the floors, and she seemed normal, but that last week before she left . . . I tried to tell her things, about having dinner or maybe going to bed, and she wouldn't even see me, or hear me, it felt like.'

'She took her address book, but she never said anything at all?'

I didn't know which would be worse, if she had left in that hazy not-my-mother state, or if she was normal when she left, and might have known that she was leaving me behind.

'No. She never talked about . . . them, either.'

Gram considered me for a moment. 'Do you want to?'

'What?'

'Talk about them.'

I lay down with my head on the pillow and faced the wall.

'We don't have to talk about them,' Gram said gently. 'I do need your help to find your mother, though.'

'No,' I said.

'No?' Gram asked.

'No!' I said again, shouting this time, sitting back up. 'I don't want to help you! I don't want to know where she went or why!'

'It wasn't the right thing, what your mother did to you, but . . .'

I could tell Gram was trying to keep her voice steady. She was getting angry. Maybe it was at me, but maybe it was at Mom.

'Don't be mad at her!' I yelled.

'Aubrey, honey, it sounds like you are mad at her.'

'You don't understand,' I said. 'Leave us alone.'

Gram stood up from the bed. She picked up the laundry basket and left the bedroom.

When Gram asked what I wanted from the grocery store, I told her I was fine, thanks. She went anyway. She bought lots of food, and when she came back she started making dinner. Dinner smelled so good I couldn't help opening the door to my room and letting the smell of baking chicken float in. When I heard plates and silverware being set on the table, I came out.

'Hungry?' Gram asked. I answered her by sitting down at the table. She had made plenty of food: a whole chicken, yellow summer squash and courgette, and corn-bread muffins. She loaded up a plate. 'You prefer white meat, right?'

I nodded. She passed the plate to me.

I tried to act like I wasn't enjoying the food too much, but it was nice to have a real meal.

'More?' Gram asked.

I nodded.

Gram didn't say anything at all about what had happened that afternoon. When dinner was over, she said she would clean up. Then she fixed me a big bowl of ice cream, vanilla with caramel on top, and sent me out to sit on the front porch. It was hot out and my dessert melted fast, but the cold ice cream felt good.

Gram kept making phone calls, learning nothing. She didn't ask me to help again with the looking-for-Mom business, and I didn't volunteer. She didn't even make me help when the police came to ask questions; she just told them what I had said about Mom leaving.

I parked on the couch in front of the TV and numbified my brain.

'Don't you have friends to play with?' Gram asked.

'Nope,' I said.

'You used to play with lots of kids.'

'Yeah, well . . . they started treating me different. It wasn't fun any more.' After that chocolate-ice-cream incident with Pennie Layne, even my best friend, Maggie Rose, had decided I was – as she put it – crazy as ants on a Popsicle.

After that, Gram didn't try to make me do anything. She let me sit in the living room, on the couch that had her bedding on it, because that was where she was sleeping at night.

I listened to her talking on the phone. She kept calling my aunts and uncles on both sides of the family, and even those dumb church ladies. Mostly, I'd hear her talk about Mom, but then I heard her talk about me. I was pretty sure she thought I couldn't hear her from the living room. But I did. I got up and went to the kitchen doorway to listen better.

'Aubrey needs . . . I mean, I don't know . . .' She was having a hard time talking. 'I just don't think I can take care of them both, Aubrey and Lissie . . . You would? . . . You would? . . . That would help so much.'

I didn't know who she was talking to or what she was planning. I couldn't stand it. I walked into the kitchen and slammed against one of the chairs as I walked by. It made a big noise hitting the table. Gram looked up, startled. I went in my room and shut the door. I put on my waltz music and lay down on my bed.

An hour later Gram came into my room. Her eyes were red. She must have been crying.

I got off the bed and turned the music up. I put on my Disney World visor and got my softball and started tossing it against the wall and catching it.

Gram looked as if she wanted to say that I was going to hurt the wall, but she didn't. Instead, she said, 'Sit down, Aubrey.' When I didn't listen, Gram said again, with an edge to her voice, 'Sit down.'

I sat, but kept tossing the softball up and down. Gram took it from me.

I folded my arms over my chest as she left the room. By the time she came back, my door was locked and I was in bed with my sheet pulled over my head, even though it was a hot night. I blocked out the sound of Gram's knocking on the door by listening to my music first, and then the loud crickets and cicadas outside my window.

I couldn't stay shut in my room forever. The first reason was because I had to pee. The other reason was because Gram made fried eggs and bacon and toast for breakfast and it smelled really good. I broke down and opened the door. Neither of us said a word as I ate breakfast.

Gram spent almost all day on the phone again, and I spent almost all day in my room. I expanded my castle drawing onto more sheets of paper and started taping them to my wall. I opened my favourite book about the Middle Ages and copied some of the things from the pictures. I drew the stables and the banquet hall. I made the walls really thick, in case of enemy siege towers and battering rams.

'Aubrey? Can I come in?' Gram asked in the late afternoon, pushing my door open.

I finished taping up a new piece and shrugged.

'Sit down,' she said, but she said it kindly, not like she had the night before. I nodded and sat; she sat next to me and took my hand. Her hand was surprisingly soft for someone who liked to wash dishes so much. She smoothed my hair with her free hand.

'Everybody's going to help us look for your mother. They're going to help us find her.' She kept her fingers in my hair even though I didn't say anything. 'Did you know that your parents picked someone to take care of you if anything ever happened to them?'

I shook my head slowly. 'Who?'

'Me,' she said.

'Oh,' I said. After I had been so horrible over the past few days, she was probably going to decide she didn't want me, either. 'I'm fine,' I said. 'I'll be fine here by myself. I like it.'

'You can't stay here,' she said.

'What am I going to do, then?' I asked.

Gram squeezed my hand and got up from the bed. 'I'm taking you home.'

3

Gram woke me up in the morning by climbing into my bed and telling me a story. I didn't hear the beginning of it, just the middle.

'So this child named Aubrey was the bravest of children –'

'Why?' I interrupted. 'What made her so brave?'

'I'm not sure. I think it had something to do with her heart.'

'Yeah?'

'She wrapped it up in cellophane, to keep it fresh for later.'

I didn't know whether to laugh or not, so I just said, 'Gram.' She seemed done telling the story, now that I was up.

'Today we are going to go on a great adventure.'

'Yeah?'

'Of course. We are going to go to Vermont.'

'Oh,' I said. 'I don't feel like an adventure.'

'Well, you can't avoid having them. It seems to me you just had a big adventure, taking care of yourself.'

'I guess,' I said. 'What about Sammy?'

'Of course Sammy may come too! Everything you need can come with us.'

I wondered if I could pack a big box of cellophane.

It turned out everything I needed had to fit in three bags. One for Gram to carry with her own bag, and two for me to carry. I didn't have any luggage, just a backpack. Gram said to take something from Mom and Dad's room. She was busy, for some reason believing the house had to be clean before we left. While she scoured the kitchen counters, I went upstairs to my parents' room.

I stood outside their door for a minute, my hand frozen on the knob. I hadn't been inside since she left. Finally, I pushed the door open and crept quietly into their room. When I opened the closet where Mom and Dad had kept their suitcases, Mom's was already gone. Some of her shirts were missing from the hangers. Her dresser's top drawer was open, the underwear drawer. It was empty.

I shut the drawer and stared at the picture of our family on the dresser. It was from last summer's town picnic.

Savannah is six, I am ten. I'm poking her, just for fun, and she is smiling, hanging on to Dad's leg. Dad has his arms round Mom, and she leans back to rest against him. If you wanted to split us all up, you couldn't, because you couldn't tear just one of us out of the picture without ripping someone else.

The picture slid easily out of the frame. I wanted it but I didn't want to look at it right away. I found an envelope in Mom's stationery drawer, tucked the photo inside and sealed it. After taking Dad's small suitcase with wheels and his duffel, I went downstairs. I was carrying too many things at once, so I dropped the envelope on the kitchen counter, and went into my room to pack.

The train station was an hour away. Gram called a car service. A car came and parked in our driveway. The driver was nice, an older man named Stan who said he 'apperciated our bizznezz,' and that he and his wife could go out to dinner as a treat because we had called. He told us that while he put our bags in the trunk.

I held Sammy myself. He was inside a plastic bag, inside his fishbowl, inside a plastic-cloth camera case. I could hold the case on the train and open the plastic bag for him to get air. I also held my pillow. I pressed my face into it because it smelled of home and my own bed, and me, I guess.

Stan held open the door to the backseat for us.

'Gram,' I whispered. 'I can't.'

'Come on, duckling. It's okay.' Gram took my elbow and guided me off the porch steps to the car, and made me climb into it. She sat right next to me, continuing to squeeze my elbow. We put on seat belts. I looked out of the window, silently saying goodbye to my house, which was locked up and empty. I wondered if Jilly was still inside, or if even she had left.

The driver dropped us off at a small platform along the side of the road in the middle of a town. The platform had a little house for the ticket seller, a restroom and a pay phone. I stood on the platform with the luggage and Gram bought us tickets. One-way tickets north.

'We're going to be on this train overnight,' Gram said. 'Then in the morning we have to change trains in New Haven to get on the special Vermont line!'

She announced the plans with excitement. I wondered if that was excitement in my stomach. If it was, it felt just like wanting to lean over the tracks and throw up. Nervous sweat wet my forehead. I had to sit down and hold my stomach.

I was sick of feeling sick all the time.

'Here.' Gram handed me a train schedule with my first ticket tucked inside. 'I'm going to go use the ladies' room. I'll be right back.'

I opened the train schedule. I started reading train times. Ours would come at 5:30 p.m. I looked at our path north. Then I read the opposite side, which showed the same train line going south. To Georgia. Where Dad's family was from. We used to live there too, until I was six. I followed the list to the stop – Savannah, Georgia – where my sister was born. I stared at her name in bold on the train schedule. Savannah.

I slid my ticket out of the schedule and held it in my hands. I tried to read the information on it, but it was all blurry. I found a little notch in the edge of the ticket and pulled at it.

By the time Gram got back from the bathroom, I was sitting with a pile of stiff paper shreds.

'Aubrey!' she exclaimed when she realized what the blue paper bits were.

She was going to kill me. I knew it.

'I didn't mean to,' I said, my voice shaking. 'I don't know what happened.'

Maybe she would yell at me, I thought. Maybe then I could yell at her again, and blame everything on her.

She scooped up all the pieces. When she spoke, it was softly. 'Aubrey, you can't stay here.'

I couldn't agree with her, but I couldn't argue with her, either. I took three deep breaths. Gram took out her wallet, which was fatter than I would have expected. She counted out four twenty-dollar bills and handed them to me.

'They won't replace a ripped-up ticket. You'll have to get a new one. Go inside and tell the man you need a ticket to New Haven on the next train.'

My feet shuffled, but they went. They walked me into the little house and up to the counter. My mouth mumbled, 'One ticket to New Haven on the next train, please.'

Gram didn't say anything about the money I'd wasted. She just took my hand when I came back to the platform and said, 'Everything's going to be okay.' When I shook my head, she added, 'Think of this as a trip. Just a grandma and her girl, off on their adventure.'

I took more deep breaths. *An adventure. An adventure. Just a little trip with Gram. Kids could go on trips with their grandparents for any old reason.* I was beginning to calm down.

When the train came, we hauled our bags on board. I wondered if we'd have to pile them in our laps, but there was plenty of room on the shelf above our seats.

I had never ridden on a train like this one before. The seats were big, with tray tables and footrests. Each car had a bathroom, and there was a dining car. I relaxed as I watched Virginia roll by the windows. The tracks were lined with towns and houses. I wondered what it was like to live along the tracks like that.

I took out my book and my headphones. I held Sammy's bowl in my lap. After a few hours we passed through Washington, D.C. We didn't really see all that much of the city from the train.

After it was dark out, we went to the dining car. They

served hot food! A picture menu hung above the counter where you paid and picked up what you ordered. We got hamburgers. They came in little plastic bags that the attendant heated in a microwave. We sat down in a booth, and about ten minutes passed before I could even hold my burger because it was so hot. It was a little soggy from all the steam that had collected inside the plastic bag. I peeled off the bun and squeezed three packets of ketchup on it.

I watched Gram eat her burger.

'Have you eaten on a train before?' I asked.

'Yep,' she said. 'On the way down.'

'What did you get?'

'Pizza.'

'Was it good?'

'It was hot. If you are hungry again later, you can get one.'

That sounded good. I would have to remember to get hungry.

'Gram?'

'Yeah?'

'Is it weird to eat kid food?'

'Kid food?'

'Yeah. Squishy burgers and squishy pizza from the microwave?'

'What's kid about it?'

'I don't know, it's just plain and soft.'

'Old-people food and kid food are the same thing. Think about it. Baby food for babies. One day someone will feed me mush off a spoon again. This squishy food is all just part of the fun of riding on the train.'

'You're not that old, Gram,' I said. She had grey hair and sun wrinkles, but she could still carry around all that luggage without complaining.

'Sixty-six, don't you forget it. Until my birthday,' she said. 'Then, add one.'

I suddenly remembered the photograph I'd left on the kitchen counter. 'I forgot . . .'

'What did you forget?'

'Oh, nothing.'

'Anything you forgot we can replace when we get there,' Gram said.

I doubted it.

There were fewer passengers on the train after dinner. Gram moved to the seat across the aisle from me and told me to try to get some sleep. I was happy I'd brought my own pillow. I nestled it under my head and curled up on the seat. I fell into a funny sleep for a while, then Gram woke me up again.

'New York City,' she said, pointing out my window.

I had never seen New York before, and was glad she'd woken me up. The string of glittery lights across the water stretched on for a very long time. I watched it until it disappeared, and then I fell back into a dreamy sleep. Once I woke and looked out of the window to see water lit up by the moon, and another time I looked out to see what I thought was forest.

In the morning Gram woke me up with a cardboard tray of breakfast.

'Breakfast in bed,' she said. It was another hot sandwich in plastic. HAM-EGG-CHEESE CROISSANT, the label said. She had also bought me a plastic cup of orange juice with a foil lid.

A few minutes before we got to New Haven, Gram had us collect all our things so we'd be ready to get off the train. This station was bigger than the one in Virginia. There were lots of platforms and many trains coming and going. Gram said that we had a while to wait for our next train, so she let me curl up next to the luggage and nap, and after a while she bought us turkey sandwiches. The morning air was cooler than it had been in Virginia, and it felt like it rushed through my nose when I breathed. That made me feel like I had a little bit of a headache.

When our next train finally came, I was ready to get on. I settled down in the seat and watched out of the window. We passed towns and woods and farms. The day was sunny, so everything looked bright and leafy green. The ride took almost the rest of the day.

As we got closer to Gram's house, I thought more about what it would be like there.

We used to fly to Montpelier to visit Gram, but I had never been there on my own before. I remembered Gram's house crowded with aunts, uncles and cousins. In the summer there would be cookouts, with as many hot dogs and burgers as you wanted, and watermelon and softball and sprinklers. In the winter it snowed, and we used to make snow angels and snowmen. If all my cousins were there, there would be a whole heaven of snow angels on the ground. There were always so many people it was hard to find a place to sleep inside the house. Savannah and I used to have to squish on the couch.

As we pulled into the station near Gram's house, I began to feel sick to my stomach again.

I clung to Sammy's bag tightly as we stepped off the train.

'We'll get you some fresh water soon, Sammy, and set your bowl up, and then you'll feel at home,' I whispered.

I knew this fact about fish, though: they don't like being tossed from one pot of water into the next.

Vermont

4

Vermont smelled like cows.

Virginia had smelled like cows too sometimes, but not like this. Vermont had those dairy cows, black and white. For some reason their odour hung in the air, and all I could smell was cows. I didn't remember the smell from visiting Gram before. It made me nauseous as we drove from the train station to her house.

'Vermont stinks,' I said.

Gram had nothing to say to that. I looked down at my shoes.

I held on to Sammy's bowl. That would be awful, for his bowl to spill in the car. He would flop around on the mat, and probably die there.

I almost asked Gram to pull over.

Soon we reached her yard. Her driveway was gravel under the trees. Her house, from the outside, was what I remembered: three stories, grey, with a wraparound porch.

'We'll get your stuff out of the car later. For now, let's just get inside.'

We'd always left our stuff in the car when we first got to Gram's. Savannah and I would dash across the yard, fly up the front steps and meet Gram on the porch. She would hug us both, one on each arm. '*Oof! My girls!*' she would say as we knocked her over. We would giggle, Savannah and I. Mom would come up next, stooping to kiss Gram on the cheek. Dad came last. He would wrench us out of Gram's arms and help her up, giving her a hug on the way.

I walked up to the porch with Gram beside me. I looked sideways. Gram's face was wet. I stood in her doorway, and threw up.

'I'm sorry, Gram,' I said. I was in bed, in one of the upstairs rooms, the one where Aunt Melissa and Uncle Steve usually stayed when we were all at Gram's.

'Now, now, duckling,' she said. 'Don't be sorry at all. I took care of your fish. See.' I saw Sammy's bowl on the night table next to the bed. 'I set his old bag of water in the fresh water so the temperatures would balance out and it won't be so hard for him to adapt.'

'Thanks,' I said.

'You're tired from your trip. You don't realize how achy a night and a day spent on a train can make you.'

I wanted to close my eyes and sleep and sleep and sleep. Was that really from the train ride?

Grown-up people complain a lot more about aches than kids do. I wondered if Gram was very tired from her trip on the train overnight.

'I'm sorry,' I said again. Gram must have heard the shakies in my voice.

'No more tears. For either of us,' she said. 'Go to sleep. I am going to. I made you a snack tray in case you get hungry.' I noticed the tray on the night table held a glass of grape juice and a plate of crackers and cheese.

I woke to bright sunlight and the sound of luggage being dragged into my room.

'Gram?'

'You have important things to do today! I made you a list,' Gram said.

'What?' I couldn't remember the last time someone asked me to do something. Well, I guess Gram had told me to pack, but before that . . . in April, it must have been . . . *Make sure Savannah is ready for the car ride . . . shoes tied, sweatshirt on, that she went to the bathroom . . .*

Gram left the list on my night table. I read it after she left the room.

1. Unpack.
2. Talk to your grandmother.
3. Spend time outside.

I looked around the room. It was really plain. The furniture – bed, dresser, night table – were all wood. The bare floor had a red oriental rug on it. There was one window, which showed the garden below with its yellow grass, empty picnic table and ashy charcoal barbecue. Gram had a vegetable patch with tomato plants, but they looked dry. I could see through the yard to the neighbours' house. They had one of those toddler climbers, some bikes, a swing set and a tyre swing in a tree. I didn't remember kids living next door.

The crackers and cheese still sat on the night table, the cheese limp and sweaty. I figured it was still good because people ate cheese in the Middle Ages and they didn't have refrigerators, so I ate some and drank all the warm juice.

I opened the top drawer of the dresser to find it stuffed full of pictures and papers. I opened the middle drawers, which were empty. The bottom drawer had three small white dresses in it.

'Gram! There's already stuff in the dresser!' I yelled. She didn't hear me.

I shut the lower drawers and went back to the top drawer. I scooped up a handful of photos. I knew they had been rummaged through before, because there seemed to be no order to them.

Gram had four children: Aunt Melissa, Uncle David, Aunt Linda and my mom, Elizabeth. The photos were all of them.

Four rusty-haired children sit under a Christmas tree. A

boy – Uncle David – plays a clarinet. Two girls hurtle down a metal slide. A girl plays in leaves. A girl blows out birthday candles. A baby grins without teeth.

It was harder for me to tell the girls apart when they were alone in the photos, but when they were together I knew Mom was the smallest. I looked back at the Christmas photo. The smallest girl was smiling, her grin showing gaps in her teeth. For someone so little, her hair seemed heavy, straight and dark.

My own hair was a faded blonde colour. It was always thin and limp. Not shiny. Savannah's hair had been like that too, but hers had been blonde. It was Dad's family who were blond and feather-haired.

I shoved the photos back in the drawer and shut it. I crossed my arms and sat on the bed. I didn't live at Gram's. I wasn't unpacking. I took my three bags and pushed them under the bed. I realized I had been wearing the same clothes for days, so I unzipped one bag just enough to pull out fresh shorts and a clean T-shirt. I changed into them. Then I sat on the bed, waiting, staring at the ceiling, thumping my feet on the floor. I thumped them one hundred and two times.

'Aubrey!' Gram called. 'Are you ready to come down?'

'Yes,' I said. She probably hadn't heard my reply. I went downstairs anyway.

The kitchen smelled really good. I even forgot about the smell of cows. Gram had made ham and scrambled eggs and toast and cantaloupe melon.

'Sit,' Gram said, and she fixed a plate for me. I sat at the table, and noticed the rooster clock on the wall.

'It's two in the afternoon?' I asked.

'Isn't that amazing?' Gram said. 'Who knew where the day went? You slept through the entire morning.' She slid a second plate onto the table for herself and sat down.

I started to eat slowly, picking at things, cutting things that didn't really need cutting, respreading the butter on my toast . . .

'What's next on your list?' she asked me.

'Talk to your grandmother,' I recited.

'Right,' she said. 'I just wanted to let you know what's going on. Uncle David went down from Boston to take over looking for your mom. The police will be looking into whether she's used her credit cards or been to an ATM, or checked into a hotel. That should give us some hints as to where she might be. And your aunts are putting together lists of friends that she might stop to see.'

'Super,' I said. 'Is that all?' I set my fork down and pushed away my plate.

'I was wondering if you'd like to see your aunts. They'd like to see you. They both live within a couple of hours' drive. We could have a summer get-together, like we used to.'

'No thanks,' I said. I didn't want to see anybody.

Gram looked like she was trying to think of something to say. I turned away from her.

'Back to your list?' Gram asked.

'Number three: spend time outside,' I said.

'Right. You need some sun and air.'

Air that smelled like cows.

There was a door in the kitchen, but I walked to the front door instead. I sat on the porch swing. A black and white cat circled some empty food dishes on the porch, then hopped up on the swing next to me. Gram hadn't had a cat last time I was here.

'Hi, kitty,' I said. I reached to pet her, and she stretched lazily along the bench. 'What are you called, cat?'

The cat didn't know, it seemed, or she decided not to tell me. She batted at my shoelace, decided she couldn't get it after all, and gave up.

The back door of the neighbour's house opened and a girl came out. She looked about my age. She had thick orangey-blonde hair pulled into a high ponytail that hung down her back. She went over to the tyre swing and hung through it on her stomach for a while. Then she got some chalk and started drawing on the grey stones behind her house. I don't know how long I watched her. Then she looked up, saw me and waved. I went back inside.

I could hear Gram on the phone. She was describing my mother.

I thumped up the stairs loudly as I went to my new room.

Dear Jilly,

  You know, I sort of thought to look for you
when I was all by myself. But I didn't really know
where you would be. You were always more
Savannah's friend than mine.

  I know Savannah was always talking about
going on fun trips with you. She used to pack
backpacks for them. You probably would have
liked the train ride I just took. It was two trains,
actually. Gram came to Virginia and picked me
up, and then we took the train up to her house
in Vermont. We saw just about everything there
is to see — ocean, forest, farms and cities. We
ate dinner and breakfast on the train and even
slept there.

  I got a fish named Sammy. He's blue but
when he wiggles his fins you can see they have a
little bit of purple on the edges. There is a cat
here at Gram's. There is also a girl next door, but
I haven't met her yet.

  I'll tell you more later.

                                    Love,
                                    Aubrey

PS I'm sorry I left without telling you.

5

For someone who had brought me to live with her, Gram really seemed to want to keep me out of the house.

'It's good for you,' she explained.

Every morning Gram handed me another list.

'Summer's not about having a list of things to do every day!' I groaned.

I looked at the new list.

1. Feed the pets.
2. Hang up laundry on the line to dry.
3. Tend the tomatoes.
4. Water the flowers.
5. Sweep the porch.

I dressed, had a bowl of wheat flakes and bananas, and checked the list again.

Feeding the pets was easy.

I dropped a food pellet into Sammy's bowl and wiggled my fingers at him. He wiggled his fins back at me. 'Sammy, you're my bestest fish friend,' I whispered to him. He wiggled back that I was his bestest people friend, which made sense, because I fed him and talked to him, and no one else ever did.

Downstairs, I put a scoop of dry food and a spoonful of canned food in a little cat dish and carried it to the porch. Gram told me she calls the cat Martha. Martha didn't spend all her time on the porch, but she did wait there every morning for her food. She rubbed against my legs when she saw me with the food dish. I took the dirty bowls back inside, then cleaned the water bowl, refilled it and brought it back out.

Gram had already washed the laundry. I didn't understand why she didn't get a drier, but she said she never really needed one. I hauled the heavy basket of wet clothes to the clothesline in the yard. I didn't like hanging up our underwear for everyone to see. Not that there were that many people around, but still.

The girl next door was around. I looked past my underwear to her, and gave her an embarrassed half-smile apology. She smiled back, and then returned to the skipping-rope lesson she was giving her little sister. Her sister must have been about four. She still had baby curls. I knew a baby-baby lived in the house too, because I had heard one crying.

I took the empty laundry basket into the kitchen. Gram was sitting at the table, head in her hands.

'Hey, Gram,' I said. I didn't want her to know I had caught her like that, upset.

'Hey.'

I put the laundry basket on the washing machine in the pantry and poured myself a glass of raspberry lemonade from the pitcher in the fridge. I sat down at the table with her.

'Who's the girl who lives in the other house?'

Gram looked as if she was coming back from far away, but then she seemed excited. 'Bridget? Oh, have you met Bridget? She's a nice girl. I was hoping you would meet her.'

'I haven't met her, just seen her.'

'Yes, that's Bridget. Bridget and Mabel, and Danny, I think, is the baby. They moved here during the winter.'

I finished my lemonade. I headed back outside to finish the list. Number three, tend the tomatoes, was my least favourite of the jobs Gram liked to give me. I had to pull out any weeds that grew in the rows between the plants, straighten their cages, mix the plant food in the watering can and water them. The whole thing probably took about an hour. My knees got dirty and my ponytail fell out, and when I went to fix it, I got dirt in my hair and on my face. Gram said it would be worth it, though, when we had great tomatoes to eat at the end of the summer. The plants seemed healthier now. They were green and full, with hard tomatoes the colour of lime juice budding under hairy leaves. As I worked, I glanced up every now and then to see if Bridget was still outside. Sometimes I caught her looking at me.

Watering the flowers was more fun. I got to hook up the hose and spray all the flowers along the house and throughout the yard.

The last job was easy. I got the broom from the kitchen pantry and swept all the dirt off the porch into the bushes and grass beneath. That only took a minute.

When all my chores were done, I got another glass of lemonade and flopped onto the porch swing to rest.

When I had finished my drink, I looked across the yard. Bridget was still there, by herself now, sitting in the tyre swing. I told my legs to stand up, to walk, but they seemed to take a long time to listen. Finally, I managed to walk myself off the porch, past the tomatoes, through the trees and into Bridget's yard. By then she was on her stomach, spinning slowly with her feet on the ground.

'Hi,' I said.

She looked up. 'You have a scar on your head,' she said.

Usually, people stare, or they ask, 'How did you get that awful scar?' Bridget made it sound normal.

'I know,' I said.

'I have one on my knee.' She pushed up her legging capris to show me. She had a big scar, pink and raised, across her kneecap. 'I got it falling out of a tree over there.'

I looked, but with the woods right behind us there

were hundreds of trees. 'I'll show you,' she said. 'It's a cool old tree.'

We left her yard for the woods. The tree felt very far away. It was a neat tree, gnarled, crooked, perfect for climbing. Bridget hoisted herself onto a lower branch and said, 'See, I started off just here, and climbed there, and then there . . .' She pointed at higher branches. 'And see that one? That's the one I fell from.' Bridget dropped back to the ground.

'Cool,' I said. She looked at my scar again, but didn't ask about it. I guess she was giving me a little room to tell her, if I wanted to.

When I didn't, she said, 'Come on.' We walked back to her house. 'I just turned eleven last week,' she said. 'How old are you?'

'I'm eleven too,' I answered.

'I'm Bridget,' she said.

'I know,' I said. 'I'm Aubrey.'

'I know,' Bridget said.

When we got back to her yard, Mabel was there.

'Bridgie, you left!' she said.

'I came back,' Bridget said. 'But I can't play with you. I'm going to play with Aubrey.'

Mabel pouted to the point of tears. It was clear she was going to start wailing soon.

'*Aubrey, can I play with y'all? Please? Please?*'

'*Go away, Savannah! You're too little!*'

'Aubrey!' Bridget hollered at me. 'Are you okay?'

'Can Mabel play?' I choked out.

'What?'

'Can Mabel play with us?' I asked again.

At first, I thought Bridget was going to get mad and say to forget the whole thing, that she didn't want to play with either of us. But instead she said, 'Okay.'

She took one of Mabel's small hands, and then reached for one of mine, squeezed it and repeated, 'Okay.'

Dear Jilly,

I said I would write to tell you some more. You always liked animals — remember when you had the pet giraffe? — so I will start with them. The cat's name is Martha. I am in charge of taking care of her now. I feed her every day. Sammy is still good. Sometimes he swims, sometimes he just floats with his fins resting and waving a tiny bit. He seems to be okay here after the move.

The girl next door is Bridget. We're the same age. How old are you now? I have trouble keeping track, but you must still be seven.

Gram is look-look-looking for Mom. I don't know why. I don't care where she went. I guess Gram is worried because she is Mom's mom and she has to be, but maybe that can't be it, because my mom doesn't seem to be worried about me. That's fine, though. I don't want to see her.

Love,
Aubrey

6

In the morning I took the envelope for Jilly and snuck outside with it before Gram could see me. There didn't seem to be anyone up at Bridget's, either.

I remembered the way to Bridget's scar tree on my own. When I got there, I stood at the base of the trunk, looking up. I had never been that great at tree climbing.

I put Jilly's letter in my teeth. I looked for the lowest branch and started my climb there. It took me a long time to get anywhere, because on each branch I stood very still for a minute and wondered how scared I was to go higher. Sweat started running down my face and my hands got slippery, but I kept climbing. Finally, I felt I'd gone high as I could go, so I carefully sat down. I took Jilly's letter out of my mouth and set it on the branch against the trunk of the tree. That seemed to be the right thing to do with it. Then I climbed back down.

Vermont wasn't as hot and sticky as Virginia, but it could still be really hot. When it was, Gram shortened my list. One morning she handed it to me with a bowl of watermelon chunks and said it was okay just to sit for a while first, if I wanted to.

I should have been used to it, the heat, but for some reason I felt awful. Being hot had never done that to me before.

Sitting on the porch swing, I closed my eyes. Dad used to say something about this kind of weather.

'*This heat is oppressive, Aubrey. It's oppressively hot.*'

'*What do you mean?*'

'*I mean I don't feel like doing a thing, not one thing. I might even get too lazy to breathe, if my body didn't take care of that for me.*'

'Good morning!'

I opened my eyes to see Bridget on the porch.

'Hi,' I said. 'Watermelon?'

Bridget took a chunk and bit into it. 'No seeds?'

'Nope. Too bad, though, we could have had a spitting competition.'

'What chores do you have today?' she asked.

'I just have to feed Martha and then water all the plants, especially the tomatoes.'

'I'll do Martha,' Bridget said, sitting on the porch railing. 'I used to take care of her all the time.'

'What do you mean?'

'When your gram was away in the spring. She was away for about a month, and I fed Martha. Wasn't she with you?'

Gram. Gram had been with us, in the spring. I remembered her being there after the funeral, when everyone else went back home. But she had only been with us for a few days, hadn't she?

'Was that a month?'

'Yeah. Don't you remember?'

I shook my head. 'Not really.'

Bridget shrugged and went inside to get Martha's food. I stayed where I was, clinging to the cold metal watermelon bowl. Bridget returned with the cat bowls and set them on the porch. Martha, annoyed with me for sitting without feeding her first, slunk up on the porch and started her breakfast.

Bridget climbed over the porch railing.

'Where are you going?' I asked.

She didn't answer, disappearing for a minute. I heard her giggle. Then I was wet with freezing-cold water!

I jumped off the swing, dropping the watermelon bowl.

'Feel better?' she asked, waving the hose at me. 'Let's do the watering. It'll be fun.'

Soon the ground around all the plants turned to mud, and the grass squished beneath our bare feet. We shrieked and ran, getting completely soaked. After a while Gram stuck her head out of the kitchen window to yell at us to stop wasting her water and ruining her lawn. We shut the hose off and sat down in the dry grass in Bridget's yard. The day was hotter, we noticed, now that we didn't have the hose on.

Mabel saw us through her window and came outside.

'Can I play?' she called.

'What do you want to play?' Bridget asked.

'House.' Mabel had obviously planned on us saying yes, because her arms were loaded with three dolls. 'Bo,' she said, handing one to Bridget. She held the second one to her chest. 'Janie,' she said. The third doll she held out to me. 'Brussels Sprout.'

Bridget and I laughed, but Mabel continued seriously. 'We have to find them something to eat.'

We scavenged for leaves, acorns and grass we could pretend was food. My stomach started to hurt again as we played. Mabel fixed oatmeal for her baby, and Bridget announced that she was making pizza. She got a handful of mud sauce from my yard, slathered it on a Frisbee, and started sprinkling grass cheese on it.

'What are you cooking, Aubrey?' Mabel asked.

'I don't know yet,' I said, looking at the maple leaves piled in my lap.

'Daddy, we made you a restaurant!'

'Oh boy! Again?'

A table is set, our play one. I drag Dad by the hand to sit, and Savannah hands him a menu with red-marker scribbles on it.

'I'd like a nice steak.'

'We don't have that at this restaurant, sir,' I say, the polite waitress.

'Okay.' He scans the menu again. 'Swordfish?'

Savannah the Chef looks at me, worried, then decides to take care of things herself. She whispers in Dad's ear, loudly, 'Our play food doesn't come with that stuff.'

Dad turns to me. 'What would you recommend?'

Savannah cups her hand again and whispers something else.

'I'll have a hamburger,' Dad says.

'One hamburger,' I say. 'Coming right up.' Savannah scampers behind the couch, where our play kitchen is set up.

'I need to go,' I said.

'What?' Bridget asked. She and Mabel looked up from their cooking.

'Yeah, I don't feel good.'

Bridget looked a little worried for a minute, then seemed to forget it. 'See you,' she said. As I walked back to Gram's, she and Mabel, absorbed in the game again, laughed together.

Inside, I went upstairs to change my clothes, and was going to get in bed, but it was so hot up there. Downstairs was much cooler because the porch kept the sun from getting in the windows, so I went down to the living room. I hadn't really spent much time there because it was where Savannah and I used to stay when we came to visit Gram, but I sat on the couch and turned on the TV. There was nothing on but those daytime courtroom shows, but I left it on, closed my eyes and put my head on the armrest.

*   *   *

Savannah lies beside me on the couch.

'Aubrey, you're in my space. Aubrey!'

'Shut up, Savannah. You're the one in the way!'

She jabs me in the ribs, and I tickle her back. Soon our low giggles turn to shrieks and laughter.

Savannah sees Mom come into the living room.

'Mama!' Savannah cries. 'Aubrey's tickling me!'

'She started it by being all squirmy!' I say.

Mom bends over us both, reaching her arms to pin us down on either side. She kisses each of our cheeks. Her long dark hair tickles me as the end of her ponytail sweeps past my face.

'Did you have a fun day here with Gram, girls?' she asks.

'Let's stay forever!' Savannah says.

'Forever?' Mom asks, sitting down. 'That's a long time to be at Gram's house! We have our own house.'

Savannah may want to stay, but thinking of staying forever makes my stomach feel funny. I love Gram, I do, but I would miss my room and my school friends.

Mom must see my feelings on my face. She bends close to my ear, whispers. 'We'll get you home soon, girl.'

'But I can stay forever, right?' Savannah asks.

Gram comes into the living room. 'What's all this talk about forever?'

'What's that, Aubrey? What are you talking about?'

Sweat was beaded all over my face.

'Gram . . . what?' I asked.

Gram took the remote control from me and clicked off

the TV. 'You were mumbling about something. Was the show upsetting you?'

'No,' I said, thinking. I shook my head. 'No.'

I sat at Gram's table and watched Bridget's family through the kitchen window. They were having a picnic dinner. They had stretched out two blankets, one for food, and one, it seemed, for baby Danny to roll around on. That seemed to be his big discovery in life, rolling himself over. I couldn't tell what they ate, but there was some kind of meat from the barbecue that I had watched Bridget's dad cook, and something leafy green, and bread rolls, and maybe something like potato or macaroni salad. Bridget's mom served it in scoops on their plates.

The air was rapidly cooling.

'Ah, isn't that refreshing?' Gram asked, coming into the kitchen. 'Let's get a pizza. Does that sound good?'

'I'm not hungry,' I said.

'Well, I want a pizza. You might change your mind when you smell it. I'll go pick one up,' Gram said. She called the pizza place, got her keys and headed out to her car.

I saw Bridget's family wave at Gram.

They didn't see me.

After Gram drove away, and no one was there to watch, I left my seat at the table and went to stand at the window so that I could see better, my face pressing against the glass.

* * *

The next day was cooler, thank goodness. Gram gave me a regular list of chores to do, which meant I had to attack the weeds around the tomatoes again. Bridget showed up to help me, and it went much faster than usual. Some of the tomatoes were orange now. When we finished, we washed our hands in the hose water and went to play in Bridget's yard.

After a few hours, her mother called, 'Girls, come in for lunch!'

'Me too?' I asked Bridget.

'Guess so,' she said. 'She said "girls", and we're the only ones out here.'

I hesitated.

'What's the matter?' Bridget asked. 'Come on!'

I followed her inside. The back door led to a kitchen that had a table with baby Danny in a high chair and Mabel in a booster seat, swinging her legs, and a nice mom in soft clothes with soft hair who looked just like a mom should. The way my mom used to. I squirmed my toes in my tennis shoes.

'Mom, this is Aubrey,' Bridget said. She went to the counter, picked up a peanut-butter-and-marshmallow sandwich and bit into it, getting the sticky filling on the edges of her mouth.

'Hello, Aubrey,' Bridget's mother said. Then she did something I wasn't expecting. She knelt in front of me and slowly gathered me into a hug. 'Your grandmother told me about you. I'm very glad you are here.'

I stood stiffly. I met Bridget's eyes. She was using her thumb to smudge away the stickies on her cheeks. She looked steadily back at me without seeming to be afraid to. She had known the whole time, I realized then. She knew everything.

I relaxed in Bridget's mother's arms, resting my head on her shoulder as she rocked me. When I finally pulled away, there was wetness on her shirt. Drops I didn't need to carry around any more.

One side of the table had a bench seat along the window. I sat there next to Bridget, our hips and legs touching, we were so close. We worked our way through the pile of sandwiches until I was stuffed. Then Bridget asked, 'Want to see my room?'

We washed our hands in the bathroom off the kitchen and made our way upstairs. Her room was above the kitchen and full of slanty ceilings and corners. There was a single bed in the biggest open space, and a toddler-sized bed in one corner.

'Mabel sleeps there. They're getting her a big-girl bed soon. She's been afraid of getting it,' Bridget explained.

She showed me everything important, most of which was on her dresser: a soccer trophy, a picture of her softball team from earlier in the summer, a collection of seashells from their family's trip to Maine the year before.

'You never said anything. About. Me,' I said.

'Mom told me not to,' she said, opening her jewellery box. 'See, this was from my dad when Mabel was born.' She held up a heart on a chain.

'That's pretty,' I said.

'Here,' she said, opening the top drawer of her dresser. She took out a bottle of pale pink nail polish. 'Want me to paint your toes?'

'Sure,' I said. I guess it didn't bother her that my feet were really dirty from our work in the garden that morning. We sat down on her rug. She had me set my feet on a magazine. I rested my arms on my knees, and put my head on top of them. I didn't tell Bridget, but while she painted my toes I was thinking of Savannah. She used to like her toes painted magenta, with silver sparkles on top.

Dear Jilly,

I've been spending more time with Bridget and her family. After everything happened, a lot of kids back at school started talking to each other about me like they were close to me, even if we weren't friends before. But then if I was around, they acted like I had some kind of disease, and no one wanted to be with me. Bridget's not like that at all. She doesn't ask me weird questions and she's not afraid to touch me. She makes me feel like she's just friends with me because she wants to be and it has nothing to do with what happened.

I never thought I would say this, but I kind of miss you.

Love,
Aubrey

7

'I thought we'd go visit school today,' Gram said.

'School?' I asked. I'd forgotten about school. What did that have to do with me?

Gram handed me the day's list.

1. Shower.
2. Dress in semi-nice clothes (no stains or rips).
3. Visit school.

'Why do I have to go there?' I asked, pulling the sheets back over my head.

'All children go to school,' Gram said. 'Or, at least, they should.'

'But it's summer.'

'School starts next week.'

'It what? Gram, I have a school.'

'Aubrey.' Gram sat down on the bed next to me and patted the blanket over my hips. 'I took care of everything. You're all set to start school up here. It might even be good for you. You'd be with a new set of kids.'

I didn't say anything.

'All right, then.' Gram patted me more cheerfully. 'Go shower. We have an appointment.'

I scrubbed in the shower, and shampooed, and then I rummaged through my clothes for a long time before picking out a light-blue skirt and a white blouse. I didn't really know how fancy she wanted me to dress, but there was something nice about putting on something other than the ripped jean shorts I'd been wearing all summer.

Gram talked about the school for the whole drive, but I didn't really listen. I watched the town change from what seemed like farms around Gram's to neighbourhoody clumps of houses. Finally, Gram parked the car in the lot next to sports fields and a large brick building.

'Here we are,' she said.

We walked inside. The building had that weird summer feeling, when there are no kids and just a few teachers in regular clothes wandering around. It was easy to find the main office. Gram told the secretary we were here to see Mr Pudlow, the principal. She told us to wait a minute, and called him. We sat down.

Mr Pudlow came out of his office. Even though it was

summer, he was wearing a shirt and tie. He shook Gram's hand, and then reached for mine. I watched his eyes take in my scar and then look carefully over the rest of me. I already didn't like him.

'Normally, I like to meet with our new students one-on-one, just to get a sense of who they are. So, if it's all right, I'll talk to Aubrey on her own for just a few minutes, and then we can go over any questions you may have,' he said to Gram.

Gram nodded and sat back down. Mr Pudlow brought me back to his office. He sat behind his desk and gestured towards a chair in front of it. I sat.

'Hello, Aubrey, and welcome. I hear you've come to live with your grandmother. She called down and had your records sent up from your old school, so I have that right here.' Mr Pudlow waved a folder at me. 'It looks like you excelled in math, science and reading especially. Are those subjects you like?'

'I guess so,' I answered. He was making me more and more uncomfortable. Perhaps my folder didn't include my latest report card.

'So tell me, Aubrey, outside of academics, what are your interests? Do you like to play a sport, play an instrument, write poetry . . .?'

Hobbies. Now that seemed long ago. I used to learn everything I could about the Middle Ages. I used to play soccer. I used to like to swim in the summer. Once upon a time I was interested in fishing and made Dad take me. I still liked reading, but I didn't think that was what he meant.

'I don't know,' I said.

'I see.'

He obviously thought I was an idiot.

The phone rang. 'Excuse me a moment,' Mr Pudlow said, and answered it. 'Yes, thank you, I've been waiting for this call.' He glanced at me. 'Actually, transfer them to Helen's room. I'll take it in there.' He hung up. 'Excuse me for another minute – I must take this call. I'll be right back.'

He left the office.

At first, I stared around at his books and filing cabinets and posters, but then I saw my file sitting on his desk. I had always wondered what it said about us in those 'permanent records'. I looked behind me out of the open door, but there wasn't anyone around. I got up from my chair and walked round to his side of the desk, and opened the folder.

Paper-clipped to the first sheet, my fifth-grade grades, was yellow legal notepaper showing a scrawl of black ink, with a date on it from the week before. It looked like a list.

> Aubrey Priestly comes to us from Virginia
> Survivor of car crash that killed her father, sister
> in April
> Neglected and abandoned by her mother
> Now residing with grandmother
> Sessions with school counsellor strongly
> recommended

I would have thought these notes were about someone else, except that they had my name on them. Survivor – I had never really thought of myself like that. But a neglected, abandoned child . . . I was definitely not one of those. Those stories were about other kids, not about me. I'd heard about those kids on TV and in books. My life was not supposed to be like that.

Were they the ones who decided I needed counselling? Or had Gram told them that I needed it? There was nothing wrong with me.

I was dizzy. I was really dizzy. I closed the folder and walked back round the desk and sat down. I covered my face with my hands because suddenly Mr Pudlow's office seemed too bright. Neglected, abandoned; neglected, abandoned . . .

Soon Mr Pudlow returned. 'Sorry about that, Aubrey. Now –'

I just made it to the trash can before I got sick.

Our meeting was over.

'I am so going to school.'

'Are not. You're still too little.'

'Am too. I'm going to third grade, like you. See, I have a pack-pack with a lunch and a notebook in it.'

'Backpack, Savannah. And you are not!'

Dad scoops Savannah up. 'Aubrey, she's going to ride along with you and Mom to school and then come home. Just make it fun for her, okay? Make her feel included.'

'Fine,' I say. But school isn't a game. I check my pencil case.

It has three sharpened pencils in it. I have three new notebooks, one clean eraser, a full lunch box and several folders. I'm all ready.

Mom puts Savannah in her car seat. Why does she have to ruin everything by always pretending? Why does she have to ruin my morning with Mom by coming along?

'Where were you all day?' Bridget stood over me. It was warm out, but I huddled in a sleeping bag under a tree in the yard.

'Visiting school,' I said. 'And I didn't feel good when I got home. I didn't want to play.'

'Oh.' She sat down. 'Are you better now?'

'A little,' I said. 'I'm still dizzy-feeling.'

'Ooh, I hate that,' Bridget said. 'Once, I had a fever for five days, and then even after I didn't have a temperature I was still dizzy for two more days. Dad says I wasn't used to walking around . . . But you can play now, right?'

'I don't want to,' I said.

Bridget frowned but sat down next to me anyway. She talked with me for a while, telling me about the movie she watched that morning. I felt a little better listening to her. After a while I got up and asked her to wait there.

I found Gram in the kitchen.

'Can Bridget stay for dinner?' I asked.

Gram nodded.

I went back outside and invited Bridget. She went home and asked her mom if she could stay, and it was fine. Gram came outside and grilled some chicken. She called us in to a table set with three places and barbecued chicken, green beans, mashed squash and rolls.

Gram and Bridget made polite conversation. I didn't listen to it.

I interrupted. 'Did you hear from Mom today?' I asked Gram.

It made me braver, having Bridget there. Because maybe then we wouldn't have this conversation just me and Gram. Because Bridget made me feel better. I don't know why, really.

Also, I was mad at Gram for the note I'd read. For telling people those things about me.

Gram looked at me, surprised. She lowered her eyes and poked her food. She hesitated, and then sighed. 'Not today.'

Gram asked Bridget another question, which Bridget answered, though she seemed less comfortable after my interruption. I stopped listening again. I didn't eat any more. When dinner was over, I scraped my plate into the garbage and walked Bridget home.

Back up in my bedroom, I looked at my clean clothes piled on top of the dresser and the opened travel bags I'd been pulling things out of, which were still under the bed. I hauled the bags out and dumped them on the floor, sifting through my things roughly, throwing them around. I didn't know where to put anything. I didn't want to do it.

Dear Jilly,

I guess I'm not going back any time soon. Today Gram took me to a new school here. I know you always wanted to go to school and Savannah told me you never got to, but maybe she was lying. Maybe you did go to school with her sometimes.

I'm not telling Gram this, but while I was waiting for the principal I read my file. I was scared about the things I read there. It sounded like they happened to someone else, or like someone had wrote up a nightmare and picked my file to stick it in. Ever since I read it, I've felt really sick. I can't stop thinking about it, about Dad and Savannah, and I guess Mom too. I think I've been pretending for a long time that everything's okay when, really, every day is harder.

I guess that's all I want to say for now. I'm going to be quick and send you this letter before I tear it up.

Love,
Aubrey

8

I heard the rain even before I opened my eyes.

'Whoa, Nellie, look at this downpour!'

I hear the expression from Dad enough that I don't wonder who Nellie is. Nellie isn't anybody. It's just something to say.

'Maybe it will let up. We've only got another hour and a half until we get home,' Mom says.

I moaned and pulled the covers over my head. Gram couldn't tell me I needed to get up. The plants wouldn't need water. Gram could feed Martha herself. I was staying put.

I began to fall back asleep.

'Aubrey!' Gram called.

I ignored her, and fell asleep again.

Eventually my door opened. I heard steps, but they

weren't Gram's steady ones. They were lighter, faster. The bed bounced and someone was sitting on my butt.

The intruder pulled the covers off me.

'Bridget, get off!'

'Get up!' she replied, without seeming to feel bad that I had yelled at her. 'Come and play.'

'I don't play on rainy days,' I said. I grabbed my covers back and rolled over, knocking her off me, and hid my head.

'Why not?'

'Rainy days are bad,' I answered. 'Bad, bad, bad.'

'I don't think so,' Bridget said. 'Come on.' There was a hint of pleading in her voice. 'Gram says she's coming up here in a minute to wake you up, anyway.'

'I'm staying right here,' I said.

'Me too, then,' Bridget sighed. She lifted the covers again, hopped in and tugged them over both of us. I looked at her under the soft pink dome protecting us from the rainy day.

'You're dirty,' I said. 'You probably walked here through the mud in bare feet and now Gram's going to have to wash the sheets.'

Bridget lifted her foot to our faces.

'Ew! See!'

I threw the covers off to get away from the dirty feet. We were both giggling when Gram came in. I stopped laughing.

'Good morning, girls,' she said, sitting on the bed and looking at us over the lumpy covers. 'Are you interested in breakfast in bed?'

'No,' I said.

Bridget nodded.

'Well, I'll fix some, then.'

In five minutes Gram brought up two trays. Each had a steaming bowl of oatmeal with a melting lump of brown sugar on top, and a plate of sliced bananas and strawberries. She sat on the far end of the bed while we ate. She looked around my room. It was still a big mess from the night before.

'What happened in here?' she asked.

I shrugged.

'Didn't I ask you to unpack a long time ago?'

'No,' I lied.

'Didn't I ask you to unpack a long time ago?' she repeated.

'Maybe,' I said.

'Look under your plate,' she said. I slid the fruit plate to the side.

1. Finish unpacking

'Fine,' I said. 'I'm done eating.' I stretched forward to hand the tray of half-eaten oatmeal to her.

'I'll leave the fruit for you in case you get hungry,' Gram said, setting it on the night table.

Bridget handed Gram her empty tray. 'Thanks for breakfast!'

'You're welcome,' Gram said, and left the room.

I pulled the covers back over my head. Bridget did the same, so that she could see me.

'Aren't we going to clean your room?' she asked.

'Maybe later,' I said. I almost fell back asleep while Bridget tried to lie still, fidgeted and finally gave up and pushed off the covers. She got out of the bed and started rummaging through my stuff.

'What're you doing?' I asked with my eyes shut.

'Folding clothes,' Bridget said. I peered and saw that it was true: she was making a sloppy stack of clothes out of the ones strewn on the floor. I watched her. She took the pile over to the dresser and opened the top drawer.

'Did you know there's stuff in here?' she asked.

'Mmm,' I said.

'Look, pictures.'

'Leave them alone, okay?'

Bridget ignored me. She dropped the clothes onto the bed and came over with a handful of pictures.

'Are these Gram's kids?'

'Yeah,' I said.

'Which one's your mom?'

'The littlest girl,' I said. I pointed to her in one of the pictures, one of the three girls holding dancing poses.

Bridget sat down. 'You miss her?'

I shrugged.

Bridget shuffled through the pictures. 'This set isn't that old. Who's this?'

She held out one of the photos. Two small girls blew bubbles in a driveway. They wore white Easter outfits stained with bright red-orange smudges on the knees of the tights and along the sides of the shoes.

'That's me,' I said.

'And your sister?'

'Yes,' I said.

'What's all that red stuff?'

'Mud.'

'Why's it that weird colour?'

'That's what colour it is.'

'I've never seen it like that before.'

'Oh. Well, that's what it is in Virginia. It's not like that here. Here all the dirt washes out. That red stuff never comes out.'

Bridget looked carefully at the stains in the picture.

'You have an accent, you know,' she said.

'So do you.'

'No I don't.'

'You do. You sound like a Yankee.'

'What!' Bridget exclaimed, but she was laughing. 'A what?'

'Someone from up north. Dad used to call Mom that sometimes. "Just like a Yankee," he'd say.'

She flipped through the next photos. Dad lifts two-year-old Savannah into the air on that same Easter. Mom sets the table for the fancy dinner – her favourite, ham and pineapple. I lie on my back, hands reaching into the Easter basket on my stomach.

'Your dad wasn't from here, then?'

'No,' I answered as Bridget scooched a little closer to me. 'He grew up in Georgia. He and Mom met down there when Mom was on a trip. They wrote letters when she went back home, and then she moved there and they got married.'

We were quiet as Bridget flipped through the next clump of photos. More of us. I shut my eyes and rested my head against her middle.

'Why are you called Aubrey?'

'What do you mean? My parents picked it.'

'No, I mean, why did they pick it? I used to think you were Audrey when Mom would talk about you, and then that you got the "d" backwards.'

'It's a family name, on Dad's side. His mom's family.'

'So your first name is a last name.'

'It was. But there were no more boys to pass it on to.'

'That's weird.'

'No. A lot of people do it,' I said.

'Here's you and your mom,' Bridget said. She held out a picture. I'm about seven, in a party dress, sitting in Mom's lap, leaning into her. She rests her chin on my shoulder, her cheek pressed against mine. Neither of us looks at the camera. It is like there is no one watching us, and we are all alone, together.

'You miss her,' Bridget said again. This time she wasn't asking. She looked carefully at my face.

'No,' I said.

Bridget was quiet again. I listened to the rain, which was a bad idea because my stomach started feeling funny and I felt like there was oatmeal stuck in my throat. I pulled a pillow to my chest and held it tight. Bridget put the photos down, and put her hands in my hair, and on my back.

'It's okay,' she said.

That didn't work. Words never helped anything.

I pressed my eyes closed and remembered that other rainy day, when words didn't help us . . . *Daddy, why didn't you just say it a little bit louder? Why? Why didn't you make us all stop?*

Bridget didn't say anything as I started to cry. She just listened, and kept petting me.

'I'm glad you're here,' Bridget said.

I liked Bridget, but I couldn't agree. I should have been down in my own house in Virginia, with my own family.

Then I thought I heard Bridget thinking. Bridget was thinking, *Tell me. It's okay, just tell me.*

And I thought right back to her, *No, Bridget, I can't.*

It took three hours, but eventually we got all my things in a place. We emptied the dresser and filled it with my clothes. I hung up a few of my nicer outfits on hangers in the closet. Gram said we could carry an old table down from the attic to use as a desk, so I set up my art supplies on it. Since there wasn't a bookshelf, I made a row of books on the desk and the dresser. Bridget was surprised that I had games, because I had never invited her to play any, so we played them on the rug before putting each one in the closet.

When we were done, it had stopped raining.

'We can go outside now!' Bridget said.

I looked around the bedroom, which seemed to say *You live here now*. I was fine with the idea of leaving it.

When we got downstairs, I saw that Gram had made us some kid sandwiches – plain American cheese on fluffy white bread that no grown-up would eat – and left a bowl of green grapes on the counter. Bridget and I ate standing up, and then headed outside.

As we started to cross the yard to Bridget's, we saw Mabel and her dad, playing. He had picked her up and was spinning her. She screamed with happiness.

'What's your dad doing home?' I asked.

'He took the day off,' Bridget said.

I stopped walking and shut my eyes. It wasn't Mabel I heard at all. Outside, maybe, it was Mabel's voice, but inside, I could hear Savannah.

'Bridget,' I said, keeping my eyes closed. 'I need to . . .'

'Go,' she said. 'You need to go.' She finished the words, but they sounded heavy, like it bothered her to say them. 'You're such a poop sometimes.'

'What did you call me?' But I had heard what she said. 'I am not a poop.'

'You're so mopey all the time – you'll seem fine and then you just . . . I never know if we're going to keep playing or if you're going to run back to bed.'

Mabel was still laughing in the yard. I didn't know if it was her making me think of Savannah, or Bridget being mean to me, that was making me feel so sick. And angry.

'Shut up!' I yelled. 'You have no idea what it's like!'

'How would I?' Bridget yelled back. 'You never tell me anything about what it's like!'

'That's not true!' I said. Hadn't Bridget and I just spent ages talking?

It only took me a few seconds to realize that she was right, that that whole time we had talked about dirt colours and accents and names. I had held back everything else.

'I have to go,' I said. I ran back into Gram's house and shut the door. I couldn't hear Mabel any more. But I could still hear Savannah. I couldn't shut her out.

I went upstairs to my new desk and took out paper. I was going to write another letter, but I put Jilly's name on the paper and that was all I could do. Bridget was right. I had nothing to say, to anyone. I climbed back into my bed.

9

I'm not sure why Gram let me, but I slept straight through to the morning. I woke up grumpy. Downstairs, Gram had put a bowl of bran flakes on the table, with a full glass of milk and a spoon next to it. I splashed the milk into the bowl and took two bites, then stirred the cereal until it turned to mush. I dumped it into the sink. I didn't bother to rinse it down.

Gram had left a chore list on the counter. I ignored it. Then I snatched it and crumpled it up.

Bridget was already outside. She was hula-hooping. Mabel was out there too, drawing on the slate stepping-stones in the grass with chalk. Neither of them saw me walk up.

'Hi,' I said. 'Can I play?'

Bridget shrugged.

'What's up?' I asked.

'We had French toast for breakfast,' Bridget said.

'With berries!' Mabel exclaimed.

I pictured the whole thing . . . Bridget's mom with a spatula flipping the bread in the frying pan, Bridget's dad leaning to kiss her cheek as he offered his plate, Danny in his high chair picking up bite-sized soggy bits and smashing them to his face, Mabel with syrup on the front of her pyjamas, Bridget asking for an extra piece . . .

'Want to go play in the woods?' Bridget asked.

'Sure,' I said.

'We have to take Mabel,' Bridget said. 'Mom's giving Danny his bath, so I'm watching her.'

'Sure,' I said. Danny probably had syrup in his hair.

Mabel skipped over and put her hand in mine. 'Aubrey, Aubrey, we're going to play!'

My heart started pounding as she swung my arm higher, but my arm was stiff. There were words forming in the back of my mind. I shoved them aside. My stomach squirmed.

The words pressed against my thoughts again, and I closed my eyes. Mabel was pulling me along towards the woods.

'Bridgie, what game are we going to play?'

'Aubrey, what do you think?' Bridget asked. 'We could play runaways.'

Runaways didn't sound like a game to me. It sounded like a stomach ache. But I said, 'Fine.'

'Let's be in one family. All sisters,' Mabel said. 'I'm Sheila-beila.'

'I'll be Crystal,' said Bridget. 'Aubrey?'

My. My *my my* . . .

'I'll be . . . I'll be . . .'

'Megan-began,' Mabel said.

'Megan. That's fine,' I said.

Mabel dropped my hand. '*Run!* Run, sisters! Run!'

She sprinted through the trees. Bridget took off behind her. I hurried to catch up, feeling out of breath already.

My. Sister. *My sister. My sister* . . .

'Hurry! He'll find us!' Mabel screamed. We had played this game before. Mabel had never explained who 'he' was, this chaser. It was just part of the game. You can't run away without something to run away from.

'Bridget,' I panted. 'Wait.' The words came out softly, like when I was small and had a fever and called Dad to bring me water. I would call and call, but he wouldn't come, because really I was not calling that loud, or maybe not even out loud at all.

I heard the other words, pressing, pressing.

My. Sister. Is. *My sister is* . . .

I stopped running.

Breathe, Aubrey. Breathe.

It was harder to see. There were patches in my vision, yellow and black. I squinted. It was getting worse.

My. Sister. Is. Dead.

My sister is dead. My Savannah. My only one.

The words, they were all there, and they were all true.

My sister was dead.

My dad was dead.

My mom left me.

My whole family was gone.

I couldn't breathe. I grabbed a tree for balance and opened my mouth to be sick, but my body wouldn't throw up. No, other things poured out of my mouth. Wails. Streams of spit, landing on my shoes.

'Aubrey?' a voice said from very far away.

Hurt. Hurt. Hurt. Help. This was not real, this was not real.

'Aubrey?' Then the voice said, 'Mabel, go get Gram. Hurry. Run!'

The wailing turned to screaming.

Why couldn't I find them?

My body bent, stooping to reach the ground. I clawed the dirt, feeling it.

'Come back,' I howled. 'Come back!'

'Aubrey. Aubrey,' the voice said.

We'd put them in the ground, Dad and Savannah. I just had to get past the surface, this old dirt, and put my family back together again. I could find them.

'Help me!'

'I'm trying,' the voice said. Hands reached to mine in the dirt. But they didn't dig. The hands took my hands and lifted them from the ground, empty. I started screaming again.

The hands, and their arms, reached around my middle and pressed, holding me together.

The pillow was soft, underneath, but the pillowcase was stiff and salty, and smudged with dirt. Why would a pillowcase be so dirty?

I wasn't the only one in the bed. I rolled over, saw Gram's sleeping face.

When she felt me move, her eyes opened. We looked at each other, really looking at each other's faces.

Then Gram said, 'Do you remember your grandpa?'

I thought.

A tall man. A deep laugh. Me, small, lifted high in the air. A raspberry blown on my stomach . . .

Raspberries, real ones, the fruit, in a bucket on the porch swing. I'm in a lap, eating the berries, rubbing my sticky hands clean on a white shirt. My grandpa's shirt.

He didn't have a face in the memories, but it was him. He loved me. I loved him.

'I do,' I said.

Gram thought again, and spoke slowly. 'When your grandfather died, it hurt so much. I remember feeling like I was broken. I thought that if I was broken, there was no point to getting up in the morning. It was so hard to get out of bed, to make breakfast, to take care of the house. And I thought, if I did those things, why would they matter?

'But then I realized I had other things.'

'Like what?'

'I had many other people who mattered to me, and to whom I mattered. None of them could ever be your grandfather, of course, but in the end I got out of bed again. For you.'

'Me?'

'You. Not just you, duckling, but also my other ducklings, my other children and grandchildren. I thought of how you didn't have to lose both him and me at once. So I got out of my bed. I cleaned my house. I bought a Christmas tree and presents, I started baking. And come Christmastime, you were all here again. My house was not empty any more. And my life was not empty. My life was not over.'

Gram's eyes studied me, waited for me. I blinked back at her. Our faces were so close, lying in bed like this.

'I miss them,' I whispered.

'I know,' she said. 'So do I, Aubrey.'

I forgot that, that she missed them too. That they were hers too.

'After the accident,' Gram continued, 'I was hurting again. This time, I thought, my heart is broken, but I have to be strong for Aubrey and my Lissie. It was you, again, that pulled me from my bed in the morning, even after I left you and your mother at your own house to put your lives back together. I shouldn't have done that so soon, I see that now. Now I miss Savannah, and I worry about Lissie so much I think I can't move because of the hurt, but I remember that my Aubrey is right here, in my house, and we need each other.'

She kissed my forehead, and climbed out of the bed.

'Sleep well tonight,' she said. 'And, tomorrow, get out of that bed.'

Gram left. I turned to my other side, towards the night table, and watched Sammy swim slow circles in his bowl.

There was no list for me in the morning. I woke up and lay there for a while, listening to birds and trees outside my window. A light breeze slipped through the screen. The air was fresh.

The sheets felt smooth and cool as I pushed them away. I got out of bed, and the thick summer skin of my feet brushed the dry cracks in the floorboards. I kissed at Sammy and gave him his food pellet. The pellet made a small plop as it hit the water, and the water rustled as Sammy rushed to it.

'Morning, Gram,' I said when I got to the kitchen.

'Morning,' she said, a smile in her voice. 'Do you want some scrambled eggs and bacon?'

'I'll do it,' I said. And I did. I put bread in the toaster. I mixed the eggs and poured them into a buttered pan on the stove. I set bacon in a smaller pan. I made a mess.

Gram set a bowl of raspberries on the table for me. Had she known I was thinking about them yesterday? Did they make her think of Grandpa too?

I slopped my food onto a plate, oversalted the eggs and buttered the toast. It was the best breakfast I'd had in a long time.

I made more toast, a whole pile, and stacked my dishes in the sink. I headed to the door. Gram looked up from the laundry she was folding.

'There's something I have to do,' I said.

Bridget was outside, making a house for little dolls out of sticks.

'Hi,' I said.

'Hi,' she said. She didn't look up but continued her construction.

'I want to tell you what happened,' I said, careful not to drop any toast when my hands shook.

'Yesterday?' she asked.

'No. What happened. To my family.'

Bridget looked up then. 'Okay.' She stood up and brushed the dirt off her hands.

I handed her toast as we walked towards the woods. When we came to Bridget's scar tree, we sat down.

Toast was maybe a bad choice. It was hard to choke down without a drink. I began shredding the top piece.

We were quiet for several minutes.

Bridget spoke first.

'I still come out here and climb this tree, you know. I've been higher even than when I fell.'

I took a deep breath, and another. I didn't tell her that I had climbed her tree too.

'We had a wreck,' I said.

'A wreck?'

'An accident. A car accident.'

I paused. It had been hard enough to say just that out loud, without even telling the story. But I had to tell, now.

'We never really went on vacations,' I started. 'I mean, except here, to see Gram. We never went and stayed in a hotel or anything. But Dad took a couple of days off in April, and he and Mom thought it would be fun just to go somewhere, so we drove about three hours to a hotel. It *was* fun. We stayed three days, and ate all the breakfast we wanted and played in the pool and went out to restaurants and watched cable in the room. Then on Sunday we started back. It was raining only a little when we left, so we got on the interstate. There were a lot of trucks and it was hilly, and soon the rain was just pouring down. You couldn't really see anything. I was sitting behind Mom. She was driving. The rain sounded good on the car and road and it made me sleepy. I was tired from the trip, so I put my head against the window and fell asleep. Savannah, I remember, had a colouring book out and headphones on, last I looked.

'So I was sleeping when it happened. They told me later, at the hospital, that a truck went out of control. It hit us, and crunched our car against the metal divider in the middle of the road. We flipped over. I woke up for only a second, because my head hit the window.'

Bridget interrupted me. 'Is that where your . . .'

I reached up and touched my scar.

'No, that happened on the other side from something broken inside the car.'

Bridget went back to just listening. She was sitting with her knee pulled up in front of her, her head resting on it. She looked straight at me as I talked.

'When I was awake, just for that moment, I heard screaming. I hurt all over, but I couldn't see anything. I could just feel that everything was wet. From the rain, and from my cut. There was blood in my eyes. And I could smell that I had thrown up. That's all I remember of it.'

I'd spent months not thinking of that one moment, that one terrible hour-long minute. Now I wasn't crying, and my stomach felt steady. Bridget made me brave.

'The next time I woke up, I was in the hospital. I was so scared, wondering why I was alone. I hurt everywhere, and I had bruises over almost my whole body. They told me I could visit Mom soon, but I wondered why they didn't say anything about anyone else, about Dad, and Savannah.'

'How old was she?' Bridget asked gently.

'Seven,' I said, getting close to crying. I swallowed and pushed it away. I tossed the torn pieces of toast onto the ground. Birds would eat them, and squirrels, after Bridget and I left.

'I'm sorry,' Bridget said. Her eyes were red, almost crying, but she didn't look away from me.

'Everyone came – Gram, and my other grandparents,

and all the uncles and aunts from both sides, and friends. There were so many people. That whole week after the hospital, with the funeral – and then after it – I don't remember much of it at all, just little bits: seeing the two coffins together, one big and one small. Uncle David trying to get me to eat lasagne someone from church had brought by, and I wouldn't. Realizing I was wearing nice black clothes I had never seen before that I didn't remember putting on, and wondering who got them for me. The worst – I wanted to tell Dad something. And I couldn't. Would never . . .'

I stopped talking. There was only one more part, really. About Mom.

'Mom and I . . . see, she had been driving the car when . . . I think that mattered . . . But it wasn't her fault . . . not really . . .' I couldn't finish this part. 'She's not a bad person . . .'

'I believe you,' said Bridget.

There were two pieces of toast left. I handed her one and started to eat the other, slowly, listening to it crunch between my teeth.

'Aubrey? I believe you,' Bridget said again. 'It's okay.'

She stood and held out a hand. I let her pull me up. She hugged me, and with her arm round my waist she walked me back to my grandmother's house.

Dear Jilly,

I remembered something today. I remembered that one pink rose that was left in my room after the funeral. Because I didn't know who put it there and I didn't see anyone go in or out of my room, I wanted to pretend it was from you, even though I know that doesn't really make much sense. I think that's how much I missed Savannah. I wanted to think that part of her was still around.

Now that I remember it, I wish I had brought that flower with me here to Vermont. It is still in my old room, dried somewhere.

But I guess it will be there when I get back, and I can find it then.

Love,
Aubrey

10

I told Gram I didn't need anything, but she said that wasn't true. She said I needed boots, hats, mittens and scarves for the winter, and new sneakers, and sweaters – at least three more – and a sweatshirt that wasn't so grubby, and a few new pairs of jeans, and certainly one could always use new socks and underwear, and think of all the school supplies! In other words, I didn't have a choice. I found myself sitting in the car on the way to do back-to-school shopping.

We went to these stores called 'the outlets'. I had never heard of them before, but they seemed like regular stores to me, except more crowded. Even though I had tried on everything in the fitting rooms, Gram insisted that I try it all on again when we got home, before I took the tags off.

I pulled on a blue striped shirt and a new pair of jeans and walked to the bathroom to look in the mirror.

'What do you think?' Gram asked. 'I think it looks pretty good.'

'Yeah, it's fine,' I said, turning round to look at myself from the back in the mirror. 'When does school start, anyway?'

'Oh, you know, middle of next week,' Gram said.

I walked back to my room to try on a different set of clothes. 'What day, exactly?'

'I think Wednesday.'

'No, Gram, what is the *date?*'

'September seventh.'

'No,' I said. 'I'm not doing anything on September seventh.'

I slammed the door, kicked aside my three hundred bags of new things, and climbed into my bed, pulling the covers over me tight.

From the other side of the door, Gram called, 'You can't seal that day off forever. You need to keep living.'

I turned my back to the door. Keep living, I thought. Just like Mom was doing? She had sealed off everything outside her, so I could have one day.

When Gram hadn't come back in a few hours, I had the feeling I had lost the argument. We would see when the day came. Maybe I just wouldn't get on the school bus. Maybe I just wouldn't get out of bed.

I didn't want to see my new school things. I shoved them into the closet and pushed the door shut.

I teased Sammy while I fed him. I rolled his food pellet between my thumb and index finger. He could see it. He waggled his tail and directed his bulgy eyes at me.

He jumped then, right out of his bowl, and into my hand. I screamed. I was going to drop him, and he would be squirming and dying on the floor. But he slipped off my skin and back into the bowl with a *splunk*. The food fell back in with him and he gulped it up.

I stood watching, my heart wishing to beat normally again.

Two days before school started, someone knocked on the screen door. It was Bridget, wearing a backpack.

'Let's disappear,' Bridget said.

Disappear.

'What do you mean?'

'I mean, let's go off for a day.'

'Where?'

'In the woods.'

She opened her backpack and showed me a bundle of peanut-butter sandwiches.

'Will your mom worry?'

'Nah. She made us the sandwiches for a picnic. She thought it might be fun.'

Bridget's mom knowing about the whole thing made it all right.

'Hang on a minute,' I said. I ran upstairs and grabbed an

envelope off my desk. As I ran back downstairs, I yelled, 'See you, Gram! I'm with Bridget!' I stepped onto the porch and closed the door behind me. 'Let's go.'

Bridget and I set off into the woods, past the scar tree. Bridget seemed to know where she was going. We followed a wide, well-worn path. It started to climb up a bit. Bridget grasped my hand to tug me along.

'Aubrey? Who's Jilly?'

'What?' I asked.

'Who's Jilly? It says Jilly on your envelope.'

'Jilly is . . . well, it sounds silly.'

'You can tell me.'

'Savannah had an imaginary friend named Jilly.'

'And you write to her? She's not, you know, real.'

'I know, I just . . . I don't know what it is. I just started doing it when I moved here.'

'Why?'

'I don't know. To have something from . . . before? I think things, and put them in the letter, and then I just . . . send it away.'

'Oh. Okay.' We kept walking. 'Does it help?'

'What?'

'Does it help? Writing the letter?'

I shrugged. 'I don't know. Are you going to laugh at me? You can laugh.'

Bridget shifted her fingers around mine to hold tighter.

'No,' she said without a hint of a giggle. 'I'm not going to laugh.'

With my other hand I held onto Jilly's letter.

After a little while I asked, 'Why did you want to run away today?'

'Huh?'

'Did something bad happen?'

'No.'

'Nothing?'

'No. We're not really running away – it's pretend. Mom knows where we are.'

'Yeah, I know, it's just, no one runs away without a reason. There has to be some kind of reason.'

Baby Savannah has finally fallen asleep for her nap.

'Can we play now?' I whisper to Mom.

'Sure. You hide, I'll count.'

Mom covers her eyes, turns towards the wall and, loudly but slowly, begins to count. 'One . . . two . . .'

On three, sure that she is counting, I run to the living room and crouch beside the couch, shutting my eyes tight. With my eyes closed, I'm invisible.

The counting stops at ten. I hold my breath, and wait. And wait.

'There you are, Aubrey!'

I squeal and she scoops me next to her, squirming her fingers against my tummy. 'You know, I can still see you if you have your eyes closed.'

'You hide now!' I say.

'Count,' Mom says.

I cover my eyes.

'One . . . two . . . three . . .'

After ten I open my eyes and look around.

The living room looks empty.

I check behind the couch.

I check in the coat closet.

She isn't there.

'Mama! Mama!' I call softly. I peek around the dining-room door. She's not behind it. I look in the kitchen's lower cabinets. She is not in them.

I wander, starting to feel panicked. Where is she?

I open the hall linen closet by the bathroom, but there are just sheets and towels. I pull back the shower curtain. No Mama.

I may cry. But this is a game, after all, so I keep looking. I open the door to Mom and Dad's room. There is a lump under the covers on the bed, waiting. I yell as I jump onto it.

'Aubrey!' she says, laughing, but with hints of scolding in her voice. 'Remember Savannah. Think of your sister.'

I snuggle against her.

'How about we sleep too, while Savannah sleeps?' she asks. I have given up naps and that sounds boring, but Mom sounds so tired, and if she doesn't play with me it will be no fun.

'Okay, Mama, we'll wait for Savannah,' I say, and close my eyes.

I think for a minute.

'Mom? You were playing, right? You weren't sneaking to have a nap?'

Mom peeks her eyes open at me and smiles. 'I knew you would come find me.'

Soon we heard the wet rush of moving water.

'There's a river up here?' I asked.

'It's below us,' Bridget said. We had to climb on steep rocks to see it, but she was right; on the other side of the rocks was a pleasant tumble of water. Bridget watched as I took my envelope for Jilly and found a way to climb down the rocks. I leaned over the river and placed the letter between two rocks, then climbed back up. Bridget and I watched until Jilly's letter got swept away.

Bridget opened her backpack and took out sandwiches and water bottles. After lunch we sat quietly watching the water. I drew my knees up and rested my head on them.

After some time I said, 'I need to find my mother.'

Bridget did most of the talking on the way down. She tugged my hand again, until I let go.

By the time we got back, our legs were sore, and it was starting to get cooler out.

'Want to have a sleepover?' Bridget asked.

'Okay. Where?'

'I don't know. Want to camp out?'

'In the woods?'

'In our yards.'

We decided to camp out on Gram's porch, because at least it had a roof if it rained, and if any animals came we could go right inside quick. Bridget's mom and dad said it was okay, so Gram ordered us a pizza and helped us set up blankets for padding under our sleeping bags. We watched the sky turn colours and become night. We watched the stars and fireflies come out.

Gram came out to say goodnight. She added, 'I'll leave the living-room light on to shine through the window so it won't be so dark. You girls sleep well, and by all means call for me if you need anything.'

Bridget and I chorused, 'Goodnight!'

At Bridget's house someone had left the outside light by the back door on so that she could go home if she wanted to.

When Gram was gone, Bridget turned her sleeping bag to put her head on my stomach. She let down her ponytail so that her hair lay loose across my sleeping bag. I ran my fingers through it. I couldn't help it; it was so shiny and flowy. When I stopped, I just looked up at the sky that I could see off the porch. I usually didn't take time to look at the stars. Tonight it looked like someone had blocked out all the light with black cloth and made pinholes for it to shine through. Thinking of it that way made the sky seem small and close, and different from the faraway blue of daytime.

'What's going to happen when we go to school?' I asked.

'What do you mean?'

'You must already have friends,' I said.

'Not really,' Bridget said. 'Some, but I came here in the middle of the year last year, so mostly people already had friends. And now we're moving up to middle school, so there'll be different kids. I'm glad you'll be at school with me.'

'I was afraid you'd have all these friends, and wouldn't want to be my friend too,' I admitted.

'You know,' Bridget giggled, 'I was afraid *you* would make all these new friends and not want to be friends with *me*.'

And then we both laughed, our secret worries released and cancelled out. It felt good to have Bridget there, to feel her against me. I wished to stay just like that forever, in the nice parts of summer we had shared, playing and, now, looking at the stars.

Dear Jilly,

I hadn't really been helping anyone look for Mom. She's the mom. It's supposed to be her job to keep track of me, right? But maybe she needs help, and maybe she is waiting for me. I just don't know how to help.

I start school tomorrow. I think you know what day it is.

Love,
Aubrey

11

'*It's my birthday! Get up, get up, get up!*'

Savannah's light body slams into mine, jumping, her knee bones and elbows bumping my hips and shoulders.

'Ow! Get off!'

'*It's my birthday! My! Birth! DAY!*'

'*I'll get up later.*'

'*I! Am! Seven! Seven, seven, seven!*'

An alarm clock rang.

I didn't have an alarm clock.

I sat up. I was at Gram's. She must have put a clock in my room. I groaned and lay back down.

Gram burst into the room, ran for the alarm and clicked it off.

'Didn't you hear the alarm?'

'Yes,' I mumbled into my pillow.

Gram snapped up the plastic blinds, letting in the too-bright morning.

'You have school.'

'I know.'

'Get ready.'

She left me alone.

I walked to the bathroom. I stood over the toilet, staring at the water, wondering whether I wanted to be sick. I decided I didn't.

I brushed my teeth, got dressed, gathered my school things and went downstairs.

Gram handed me two brown paper bags.

'One's lunch. The other is blueberry muffins for the bus. You'd better go meet Bridget. The bus will be here soon.'

Gram followed me out to the porch. She felt like an opposing magnet behind me, pushing me invisibly away from her without touching me.

Bridget and her family were already outside. Apparently, the bus would pull up in front of her house. Mabel ran around, shouting, 'School school school school!'

'Mabel's going to preschool today,' her mom explained. 'We're driving her there later.'

I looked for something to say. 'I brought us muffins.'

Bridget's mom looked at me, her smile fading from cheerful to sad. 'That was a good idea.'

'It's coming!' Bridget shouted.

The bus rumbled up our bumpy road. It was already full of children.

'Bye, Bridgie!' Mabel shouted, not breaking the circle

she was running. Bridget's parents, her dad holding Danny, kissed Bridget's cheeks. She boarded the bus, and her dad snapped a picture with his free hand. Bridget turned at the top step and called to me, 'Come on, Aubrey!'

Gram kissed my temple and gave a gentle push on my backpack. 'Have a good day, sweet.' Bridget's mom set a light hand on my shoulder as I climbed onto the bus.

Bridget led us to the middle of the bus, where there was an empty seat. She paused so I that could move past her to the window and hopped in beside me. We put our backpacks where our feet should be, our feet on the vinyl seat-backs in front of us. We picked at our blueberry muffins, starting at the sugar-crusted tops and working our way down. Bridget turned towards the aisle a few times to join in conversations. After a lifetime of sitting, it felt, we pulled up to the school-bus drop-off.

'You ready?' Bridget asked.

I was still staring out of the window.

'She didn't say anything about her,' I said.

Bridget didn't ask what I meant. She looked at me, then patted my bare knee. 'Come on!'

We scooted off the bus and joined loose lines of kids parading to the school building. I didn't know where to go.

'Go to the office,' Bridget said. 'They'll give you a schedule. We got ours on the last day of school.'

Bridget came with me to the office and greeted the secretaries. I mumbled my name and that I needed a schedule. One of the ladies behind the front desk handed one to me, then looked down at my name on the paper again, snapped her gum and sifted through a pile of papers.

'This is for you too.' She passed me a folded pink note.

'Uh, thanks,' I said. I opened the note. 'I have a meeting with Amy Carlisle tomorrow,' I said. 'Who's that?'

'Guidance counsellor,' the secretary answered, not looking up.

Goody.

Bridget and I left the office.

I focused on what I needed to do. I scanned the schedule: *Homeroom – language arts, Ms Engleheart, Rm 230.*

'Where are you?' I asked Bridget.

She pulled her schedule out. 'Math. Mr Holt. Room one-twenty.'

I started down the hall, seeing lockers and wondering if we would hear about getting our lockers in homeroom. I hadn't had a locker before. We passed rooms 118, 119, 120.

'That's me,' Bridget said. 'I guess I'll see you at lunch,' she said.

'Bye.'

Bridget went into the classroom and left me standing alone in the hallway. I mean, I wasn't alone, there were tons of kids running around, but I didn't know them, so I was alone.

I followed a few kids upstairs and found room 230. I didn't talk to anybody and just slid into a desk attached to a chair. I took my ponytail out for something to do, but also so that my hair would fall over my scar. That way, it wouldn't be the first thing everyone saw when they met me.

Most of the kids in the room were leaning against the desks, talking to each other. I could tell the leaning had something to do with showing they were cool. A lot of the girls had loose hair hanging in their faces. I was pretty sure they didn't have scars to hide too. Even some of the boys had longer hair. One boy was running around the room, kind of acting like a little kid. He grabbed a hat off someone's head, an invitation for a chase, but the other kid just grabbed the hat back the next time the boy ran past. One of the girls shook her head as she watched him, sighing, 'Marcus . . .'

The bell rang and the teacher came in – Ms Engleheart.

'Sit down, everyone.' She nodded to the boy called Marcus to stop running.

Some people groaned as they realized they were stuck sitting in the front of the room.

Ms Engleheart went through the homeroom business first. She called the roll, assigned locker numbers, took lunch registrations, made announcements. Then she switched to language-arts business and handed out our text-books.

'You won't need these tonight,' she said. 'Tonight you are going to do the classic first-day assignment. It will be a letter to me, to help me get to know you, and also to help you get used to writing after a sleepy vacation. Can anyone guess the assignment?'

A boy raised his hand.

'Mr Cho?'

'How I Spent My Summer Vacation,' he recited.

'Excellent. Yes. For homework tonight, please write me a letter on the subject: How I Spent My Summer Vacation.'

Super. That sounded like the best assignment ever. I decided I hated Ms Engleheart as the boy in front of me passed back the printed list of course expectations.

Dear Ms Engleheart . . . I spent my summer vacation wondering where my mother is . . .

My mother . . . Dad . . . Savannah. I hadn't thought of her, not since I'd got off the bus. I hadn't been thinking of my sister on her birthday but of other things, things that didn't matter.

I hated myself a little too.

'Bridgie! Bridgie! Listen to me about school!' Mabel shouted, running to us when we got off the bus.

'Later, Mabel,' said Bridget. 'I want to hang out at Aubrey's.'

'I'll come!' said Mabel.

'No,' said Bridget. 'Go away.'

'But I want to tell you –'

'No,' said Bridget. 'I want to talk to Aubrey about school.'

Mabel scrunched up her face, burst into tears and ran back inside.

'Go,' I said to Bridget. 'Go be nicer to Mabel. I have to do my homework, anyway.'

As I walked to Gram's, she came out onto the porch.

'How was it?'

'How was what?' I asked. My backpack was heavy with new-to-me but already old-and-used school books. I held the bag low in front of me, kicking it as I walked.

'How was it? How was school?' Gram asked, looking concerned.

'School stinks.'

Gram sighed and followed me up the steps and into the kitchen. She'd fixed a snack of crackers and cheese.

'Your favourite,' she pointed out.

'I know,' I said. I consented to the snack idea and sat down, immediately feeling better as my teeth slid slowly through the soft orange cheese and then broke the cracker with a quick snap. Gram poured a glass of cranberry-grape juice.

'Lunch was okay?'

'Yeah, it was fine.'

'Did you sit with Bridget?'

'Yes.'

Gram sat down with her own glass of juice. 'Now. Why does school stink?'

'Homework,' I said.

'Homework is normal,' Gram said. 'What do you have?'

'I have reading and questions for science, a page of

reviewy stuff for math, and a map to memorize for social studies.'

'You can handle all that.'

'And. And I have to write a letter.'

'A letter?'

'A letter: How I Spent My Summer Vacation.'

'Oh. Ohh,' said Gram again, understanding. 'You can handle that too.'

'I don't want Mzzz Anglebreath to –'

'Mzzz Anglebreath?'

I shook my head, warning her not to get mad at me right now.

'You don't have to tell her about *everything* you did this summer. Just pick one little thing to tell her. Tell her about, I don't know, riding the train or meeting Bridget. She doesn't have to know anything you don't want her to, and you don't have to write about anything you don't want to.'

Just like you aren't talking about her today, I thought.

'Gram?'

'What, sweetie?'

'Do you think you can take me to a toy store?'

'Yeah, we can go right now. I'll get my purse.'

I had money, eighty dollars, in my sock drawer upstairs. But if Gram was willing to pay, that was better, because who knew when I would be on my own again and need it.

We drove to a toy store. Gram handed me a twenty and sat in the car so that I could go in by myself. I looked and looked, up and down all the aisles, and finally I decided on a board game. It came in a container the size of a shoe box, not a flat game box. The players were princesses, and you had to collect jewels for your crown by answering questions, and make your way through a forest. It cost $12.99. The most important thing was that it said on the side of the box, *Ages 8–12*. The guy at the counter put it in a bag, and I went back to the car.

Gram didn't ask what I had bought. She drove us home. When we got there, I went to the upstairs hall closet and got the green-and-blue-striped wrapping paper out, and wrapped the present on the floor of my bedroom. I carried it downstairs to the kitchen, and set it on the table.

Gram had been at the counter having a glass of water. She put the glass down and left the room for a minute. When she returned, she carried a box wrapped in the same paper. She set it on the table next to mine.

'I've had it a while,' she said.

I didn't want her to say anything.

Savannah would walk in the door, see the presents. Shake them. Ask to open them now.

After dinner, Gram would say. Dinner would be frozen chicken fingers baked in the oven, and then white cake with pink frosting.

I fixed my eyes on the kitchen doorway, willing her to walk through it.

Try, Savannah, try. You might still be okay, if you want to be.

My eyes started to get swimmy. Gram set a hand on my shoulder.

'Aubrey,' she said gently.

'I just thought it would help, the present . . . so she would know . . . I didn't forget.'

'She knows, darling. She knows.'

I looked at the two presents. 'What should we do with these?'

'Put them in the attic,' Gram said.

I didn't question her reasoning, but I scooped up the presents and carried them carefully upstairs.

Daddy stands in the doorway. Then he bursts into a big smile, rushing into the room and scooping me up in his hands and throwing me into the air.

'She's here, Aubrey!'

'Who's here?'

'Your sister! She was born! Just two hours ago! She and Mama are sleeping at the hospital, but, come on, let's get your shoes – we have to go see them!'

I hurry to get my shoes. I am happy. I am happy to leave the neighbours' house, because they have a big, furry, barky dog and because the house smells like tacos even though no one is making tacos, but I am also happy because Daddy is so happy. I have never seen him this happy, this excited.

I grab a pink tennis shoe and shove my foot into it, but it is the wrong foot and Daddy has to pull my foot back out again and find the other shoe. When he stoops down to help me, he doesn't bend his legs enough at first and ends up falling on his bottom. We look at each other and start laughing. I jump on him, knocking him down the rest of the way. He kisses my cheek and sets me back upright. 'Hurry!' he reminds me. 'We must get to the hospital. You must meet your sister!'

We drive to the hospital. It is big and scary. There is a hallway with a big window looking on a room full of babies. Other brothers and sisters gather there with daddies and aunties and uncles, peering through the glass. Daddy hoists me up to stand on the wooden sill.

'There she is!' He points. 'Right in front of us. See her, in the pink blanket with the white stripe? That's your sister. That's Savannah.'

Dear Ms Engleheart,

This summer I grew tomatoes.

I didn't plant them myself; they were there already. But they were a little sick (yellow& droopy&dry). I watered them every day after that, and pulled out the weeds from the dirt. It was hard work and I didn't always like it.

By the end of the summer there were tomatoes. Lots of them. Some were tiny and sour tasting, but some were big&red&juicy. When you sliced them they weren't like slices from grocery store tomatoes, with a hard centre. Instead they were all shaped different inside, with lots of squiggly, seedy compartments. Some tomatoes were not red but were orange or yellow.

There were more tomatoes than we knew what to do with. We ate tomato sandwiches for breakfast, lunch and dinner. We ate tomatoes plain, like apples. We gave baskets of them to our neighbours. Gram stewed some and sealed them in jars to cook with later. We made pasta sauce. We made veggie stew. I wondered if actually there were too many tomatoes. I also wondered sometimes if I even wanted tomatoes at all, because maybe I wanted something else, like a kiwi, or bananas.

That was my summer vacation.

Love,
Aubrey

12

Amy Carlisle's office was a small room right round the corner from the main office.

I skipped science to get there at ten o'clock. The door was shut, so I waited outside. A few kids walked by, but I kept my eyes down.

The door finally opened. Marcus came out, smiling. 'Hey, Audrey,' he said, trying to slap a low five on my hand. He missed and hit my lower arm instead. 'Oops, sorry!' I didn't correct him on my name as he shoved a handful of M&M's into his mouth.

I went inside the office. If Marcus was the kind of kid who came to see Amy Carlisle, I didn't need to.

She looked nice, sitting in one of two cushy chairs, with a notepad on her lap. Her hair was straight and dark, with no frizzies, and it hung in different lengths around her face.

'Hi, Aubrey?'

'Yes, ma'am,' I said, dropping my backpack and sitting in the other chair.

'Please call me Amy,' she said, getting up and closing the door. 'Did your first day go all right?'

'Yeah, it was fine,' I said. 'Um . . . what kind of kids do you usually see?'

'Kids aren't kinds, Aubrey. Everybody is different. Everyone has his or her own stuff to deal with in life, right?'

'I guess so.'

'So sometimes some people find it easier to talk to a grown-up who's not their teacher or who doesn't live in their house. I'm here to be that grown-up to people who might want to talk a little.'

'So that's what we'll do, talk?'

'If you want to.'

'So you . . . know about me?'

'A little. But we don't have to talk about anything you don't want to.'

I kept my mouth shut, to show her this was the case, that I didn't want to talk about anything. Maybe Amy got that a lot, because she continued lightly, cheerfully.

'So you live with your grandmother?'

'Yes.'

'Do you like to spend time together?'

I hadn't thought of it like that. Not since I came to live

with her, anyway. 'I mean, we used to,' I said. 'Now it seems a little more business.'

'What do you mean?'

'She's always cooking and cleaning stuff and, you know, worrying.'

Amy nodded.

'Have you made any friends here yet?'

'Yeah.'

'Wonderful!' Amy said. 'Well, good, good. Does the schoolwork seem manageable?'

'I guess so.'

'I think the easiest way to adjust to a new school is to make sure you adjust academically and socially, wouldn't you say so?'

'Sure,' I said, feeling like it was kind of a stupid point.

'So I'd really like you to try to keep up with your homework, okay? Also, this first week I'd like you to sit with someone you don't know at lunch. Do you think you could do that?'

I nodded.

Amy wrote something on the notepad, tore off the top sheet, and handed it to me.

'That's our next appointment. I want to hear how everything goes. If you want to talk between now and then, stop by. If I'm not here, ask at the office and they can help find me, okay?'

'Okay,' I said, though I couldn't imagine looking for her before our next appointment.

'Don't forget to take some M&M's from the jar,' she said.

'Oh, I'm fine, thanks.' As I left her office, I wondered if everyone who walked by wondered what was wrong with me.

After school I was sitting at the kitchen table doing my homework when Gram came in from gardening. She was all dirty and looked like she was hot.

'Well,' she announced. 'I suppose that's the end of the garden for this year.'

She wiped her hands on her jeans and put a pot of water on to boil.

'This is the spaghetti water,' she said. 'You'll keep an eye on it for me while I go take a quick shower?'

'Sure,' I said.

Gram was gone maybe five minutes when the phone started ringing.

I stared at it. 'Gram!' I yelled. 'Phone!'

The truth was, I was afraid to answer it. But Gram seemed to spend all day either on the phone or waiting for it to ring. She would probably be mad at me if I didn't pick it up.

I ran to the bottom of the stairs. 'Gram!' I yelled again. She must have been in the shower already.

Another ring or two and the person would probably hang up. I ran back to the kitchen, held my hand on the phone for one more ring, picked it up and then clicked the Talk button.

'Hello?' I asked, hoping whoever was on the line couldn't hear my pounding heart.

'Hi.' I didn't recognize the voice, but it was a woman. 'Who is this?' she asked. She sounded extremely worried.

That was a funny question. She was the one who had called me.

'It's Aubrey,' I said.

'Oh, thank God! Are you all right? You're with your grandmother?'

'Who's calling?' I asked.

'It's Aunt Janet,' she said.

'I don't have an Aunt Janet.'

Just then Gram, who must have heard the phone from the bathroom after all, came running into the kitchen, dripping, in a towel. She grabbed the phone before I could say anything else.

I sat down at the kitchen table. At first, Gram just said simple things, like her name, and yes, and no, and a few things about me – that I wasn't by myself was one – but then she was saying 'Thank God. Thank God!' as she held her towel tightly around her chest.

My ears started buzzing. It felt like Gram was speaking in a faraway tunnel. I got up from the table, slowly, and then, moving more and more quickly, made my way up the stairs. I rushed to my bed, lay down and counted my breaths, waiting.

* * *

An hour and over a thousand breaths later, Gram came into my room, looking less wet but still wearing her towel. Her grey curls were limp around her face.

'I know where she is,' she said. Her voice sounded happy, but extremely tired at the same time.

'That's nice,' I said.

'It must be at least some relief to you?' Her voice went up at the end.

'Not really,' I said.

'Don't you want to hear where she is? Don't you want to know how she got there?'

'Nope . . . Who's Aunt Janet?'

'Aunt Janet was a friend of your mom's from college. She says you met her, when you were little. You don't remember?'

'Nope.'

'Your mom is with her.'

'Where?'

'Colorado.'

'Colorado?'

'It's where Janet lives.'

None of this news made any sense to me. 'She's . . . okay?'

'She's . . . safe,' Gram said carefully.

'I don't understand,' I said. 'I don't understand.' When Gram didn't respond, I repeated it a third time.

If she was okay, then what was she doing in Colorado? Why wasn't she with me?

'Aubrey?' Gram said.

'I'm going to be sick.' I leaned over the side of the bed. Gram looked alarmed.

'Duckling, darling . . .' Gram hurried over and lifted my head. She held me against her towelled chest. 'Take deep breaths. Everything's okay now. There's no need to be sick.' She waited until my breathing had returned to normal, then said, 'I'm going to go get dressed. We'll talk then, okay?'

I sat back against the headboard, feeling my forehead start to sweat.

Gram came back in a few minutes, dressed and with combed hair. She sat down on the bed and took my hand. 'Your mother went for a very long drive,' Gram started slowly. 'We don't think that she really had a plan. She stayed at motels, mostly, or campgrounds where it was okay to park a car for the night. It seems like she was entirely alone until she ended up stopping in at a friend's house in Colorado.'

'Aunt Janet's?'

'Yes. Janet and your mother hadn't talked in a really long time, so she didn't know about anything that had happened recently. And when your mother got there she was acting as if everything was fine, saying she was just off on a girl's adventure. When Janet asked how everything was and how you girls were, your mother said you were fine. Janet invited her to stay for a little while. But after just a few days Janet could tell that something was wrong. Your mom would sleep through the whole day. She didn't sleep peacefully; she kept calling out. When your mother wouldn't call home, Janet felt that something was really, really wrong.' Gram paused, to check how I was taking everything. I had my eyes shut, but I was listening. 'She got your mother to talk about it this morning. She realized that you had been left behind. She didn't know who to call, so she found your mom's address book in her things and called the phone number that said "Mom".'

'You,' I said.

Gram nodded.

'That's the whole story?' I asked. 'That's all you know?'

'There's a little bit more,' Gram said. 'I talked to Uncle David too. He's going out to get her. He's leaving right away. He'll bring her back to Virginia and take her to a doctor. Not the kind of doctor who checks your bones and things like that. The kind who checks your feelings.'

'I know what kind,' I said.

Gram was very quiet for a few minutes. Then she suggested, 'I could get that spaghetti water started again.'

I shook my head. 'I'm not hungry.'

'I'll leave you alone,' Gram said. She got up and went to the door. I got under the covers, as if it was bedtime.

'Gram? Do you know . . .'

Gram paused in the doorway and turned. 'Do I know what, sweetie?'

'Did she call for me, at all? You know, when she was sleeping?'

'I'm sure she did,' Gram said.

After Gram left, I felt like I had eaten a whole pot of spaghetti, and that it had turned into squirmy worms in my stomach.

'You look like you didn't sleep at all,' Bridget said to me on the bus the next morning. 'Your eyes are all red and streaky.'

She meant bloodshot. I rubbed them. I hadn't slept much. But I think around three or four in the morning, knowing I had a plan, I fell asleep for a little while. When I was asleep, I dreamed about Mama, and riding in a car way out somewhere dusty to meet her. I couldn't tell in the dream who was driving the car. Then I would wake up, and when I shut my eyes the dream would start again.

'My mom . . . turned up,' I said. 'She's in Colorado. But my uncle is bringing her back to Virginia.'

'Oh,' Bridget said. 'That's . . . good, right?'

I shrugged.

'What are you going to do?' she asked.

When Mom left, I couldn't go after her. I didn't know where she was. Now I did.

Bridget looked at me. Then she gasped. She wrestled my chubby backpack out of my arms and unzipped the main section.

'Aubrey!' she cried. She lowered her voice. 'Aubrey, *no*!'

I snatched the backpack and shoved the jeans, socks and underwear peeking out quickly back in.

'How are you planning to get there?' she whispered.

'Train,' I said. I knew that the eighty dollars in my pocket wasn't going to get me all the way there on the train, but it would be a start. 'Or the bus. There are plenty of buses in this country.'

'No,' she said.

I hadn't yet considered bicycle, but that was a good option. I could steal one at school. It would take a long time to get there, but I knew how to take care of myself.

'I have to,' I said. 'If I leave now, I can be back in Virginia by the time she gets there.'

'No.'

The bus pulled into the school parking lot. Kids started getting off. I stood up, and Bridget followed closely. When we got off the bus, she said, 'Aubrey, it's okay.'

'Nothing's okay.'

'She's safe, and you're safe.'

I shook my head and walked into school with my fat backpack. I hadn't had room in it for homework, or books, so I wasn't quite sure why I wandered to class just to get into trouble. I knew that with people coming into school it would be too hard to sneak away first thing in the morning. When I said I didn't have my homework, Ms Engleheart said to bring it tomorrow. My math and science teachers said the same thing. Well, it didn't matter, because I wouldn't be there tomorrow.

At lunchtime I didn't go into the cafeteria. Instead, I pushed open an exit-only side door and slipped outside. I went to the bike racks and started looking for an unchained bike. That could get me at least as far as the train station. If I remembered how to get there.

'Aubrey,' a voice said. I turned round. It was Amy. Great.

'What are you doing out here, with your backpack? You aren't heading home?'

'No,' I answered.

'Come inside. I want to talk to you.' Amy ushered me back inside.

Gram must have called her. I should have known.

I dropped with a thump into one of the chairs in Amy's office.

'I saw you leave the building,' she said. 'But I wasn't sure where you'd be going right now. Is everything all right?'

'I . . .' I didn't know what to say. I didn't even know if my news was good news or bad news. If it was good news, to know where Mom was and that she was okay, why did I feel so hurt and upset?

There was a knock on the door. A secretary poked her head in.

'Aubrey's grandmother is here to pick her up,' she said.

I was surprised to hear that. Had Gram heard something else? Had Mom herself called?

'I'll walk her to the office,' Amy said. The secretary closed the door. 'Before we go, is there anything you want to talk about?'

I shook my head.

Amy walked me to meet Gram in the front hallway.

They shook hands and Gram thanked her. Gram said she had already signed me out, so we walked out to the car. When I opened the door, I was surprised to see a plastic bowl with a lid on it sitting on the passenger seat.

'What's Sammy doing here?' I asked.

'He didn't like thinking he'd been left behind,' she said. 'So I told him we could catch up with you.'

I picked up his container, got in and put him in my lap. Gram got in too, but both doors were still open. Gram didn't even bother to put the keys in the ignition.

'How did you know?' I asked.

'Let's just say a nice little girl we both know told a little lie. When she found herself without her friend in the cafeteria, she said she was sick and had to see the nurse, and then she told the nurse she had to call home. Then she told her mother to go next door and tell me that I had to come to school right away, because Aubrey was going to run away.'

'Bridget?'

'Who else?'

I didn't say anything.

'I talked to her today,' Gram said.

'Bridget?'

'No. Your mother.'

'Oh.' My heart started pounding. Maybe Gram had brought Sammy because she was going to take me there. Maybe she was going to put me on a plane and send me back to my mother. 'What did she say?'

'Just that she was sorry, over and over. She *is* sorry.'

'Sorry for what?'

'For leaving.'

That wasn't what I wanted to hear she was sorry for. I thought maybe if I could just get back to her she would see how wrong she had been, and how much she loved me.

'I was thinking,' Gram started slowly, 'that maybe you would like to talk to her.'

There was utter stillness in the car, just a slow *blup blup* from Sammy, and the flutter of his fins.

I nodded.

'You would?'

'Very much,' I whispered.

'You're sure?'

'Yes.'

We shut the car doors and drove slowly home.

Only when we got into the kitchen did I realize it was such a cloudy day. Without the lights on, even though it was just one o'clock, it seemed so dark inside the house. We left the lights off. I sat down at the kitchen table.

'Gram? After, can I go up to bed? I'm really tired.'

She nodded at me as she dialled. 'Hi, Janet? Yes, it's me again. Yes . . . Aubrey would like to talk to her. In a few minutes? Sure. We'll be here. Thanks.'

Gram set the phone on the table by me. 'She's going to call in just a minute.'

I nodded, to show that I understood.

At least five minutes passed. I stayed right there, waiting.

When the phone rang, I jumped. I pressed the Talk button and held the phone to my ear. I didn't say hello.

'Aubrey?'

It was my mother's voice, but it was heavy, the way it had been since the wreck.

My heart was pounding in my ears. Maybe she could hear it.

'Aubrey, sweetheart?' she said again. 'I'm so sorry.' She was starting to cry. 'I'm so, so sorry.'

I listened. I could hear something soft like breath, and something rustly like tissues brushing against the phone.

Can you hear me, Mama? Can you hear what I am asking you?

Clinging to the phone, I listened for the answer/not-answer that she was not giving.

I don't know how long it was. Two minutes. Ten. Twenty.

I took the phone from my ear. It gave a small beep as I clicked the Hang-up button. I set the phone down on the table.

When I heard my own gasping breaths, I realized that I was starting to cry too. Then Gram's arms were round me. 'Come on, come on,' she was saying gently. She held me, and then made me stand up to go upstairs. She put Sammy back in my hands, and when we got to my room, she took the container and poured him back into his bowl. I climbed into bed, and Gram patted my hair as I cried. Then I was ready to do what I had fought against the night before, and I fell asleep.

It was even darker out when the door pushed open. A small figure stood outlined in the bright light of the hallway.

Bridget.

She stood, just waiting.

'I'm not mad,' I said. 'You can come in.'

Bridget kicked off her tennis shoes, wiggled her arms out of her coat. She left her things by the door, which she closed behind her. She ran for the bed. I lifted the edge of the blanket, and she snuggled against me.

'I'm sorry, Aubrey,' she said. 'I had to.'

'I know,' I said. She rested her head on my chest. My fingers found their way into her hair. After a few minutes I said, 'If I had gone all that way, I still wouldn't know.'

'Wouldn't know what?'

But I couldn't say. Eventually the question faded into the dark quiet of the afternoon. Bridget fell asleep first.

'Where do you want to sit today?' Bridget asked.

We stood at the edge of the cafeteria, Bridget with her tray of school lunch, me with my brown bag. Searching for a seat in the cafeteria wasn't fun, but usually we could find a table where we could sit by ourselves.

I thought guiltily of what Amy had asked me to do. I was going to see her the next day, and would have to tell her that I didn't manage to have lunch with anyone new.

That was when I noticed Marcus sitting by himself, drumming his plastic fork on his lunch tray.

'Let's sit over there,' I said.

'Where?' Bridget asked.

'There. With Marcus.'

'Who?'

I nodded towards him. Bridget raised her eyebrows. 'Why?'

'Just cuz,' I said. 'He's all by himself.' Really, I didn't know whether I wanted to do what Amy had said, but it was possible Marcus had to do things for Amy too, and so, of all the people in the crowded cafeteria, he seemed like the most comfortable choice.

'Okay,' Bridget said. I led the way over to the table.

'Hi.' He looked at me carefully. 'Au-Bree.'

I nodded to show he got it right. 'Can we sit?'

'Welcome, welcome!' Marcus said in an extremely loud voice. Bridget raised her eyebrows again but put her tray on the table and sat down. I sat down too, and took out my ham sandwich and my orange and my chocolate pudding. After his big pronouncement, Marcus had gone back to playing the imaginary drums on his lunch tray.

'You guys are in the same homeroom?' Bridget asked. Marcus and I nodded.

No one said anything for a few minutes after that.

A girl came by. She was going from table to table with a box. 'Hi, I'm Tia Fergus and I'm running for class office. Do you guys want badges?'

Marcus shrugged and Bridget said, 'Thanks! That's great.' She took a badge and pinned it onto her shirt.

'Where do you stand on the issues?' I asked.

'What issues?' Tia asked, confused.

On the inside I laughed, but I kept my face straight. 'Sure, we'll take some badges.'

Tia didn't smile as she put two more badges on the table. 'Um, remember to vote next Tuesday.'

After Tia left, I let my badge just sit on the table, but Marcus picked his up and started flipping it around. Then he opened the pin clasp and looked at the pin.

'Want to see something?' he asked.

'Okay,' said Bridget.

Marcus took his unopened can of orange soda. He set it on its side and rolled it to me. I didn't understand what he was up to, but I rolled it back. Then Marcus picked up the can and shook it. After a good minute of shaking it, he set it back down on its side on the table. He took the pin, pressed it into the side of the can, then pulled it back out.

A fountain of orange soda shot out of the can as a fizz of orangey foam slid down its side. Bridget and I laughed, and Marcus smiled a big goofy grin.

The lunchroom aide rushed over. The aide was a male teacher who did not seem to think anything about the situation was funny, even though Bridget and I were still laughing. He asked Marcus, 'Do you think puncturing a soda can is funny or safe?'

Marcus, still grinning, shook his head and saluted us as he was led to the office.

'Well,' said Bridget, opening my pudding and taking a bite with her own spoon, 'that was definitely the best lunch so far.'

I had to agree.

13

I sat in Amy Carlisle's office for the fourth time. I'd only been to our appointments, never in between, but I kind of looked forward to them.

'I spoke with a few of your teachers, and they told me you are pulling above-ninety averages in their classes,' Amy reported. 'That's wonderful!'

I wondered if she was going to follow that with 'Have some M&M's.' My eyes must have flickered to them, because Amy gave a light laugh and said, 'Go ahead. I don't mind if you have your treat a little early.'

I took the M&M's jar and put it in my lap, eating one colourful chocolate at a time.

'Have you and your grandmother been able to spend any good time together lately?' Amy asked. 'I remember you mentioning it previously, and it seemed to be something you missed from before you lived with her.'

'Not really,' I said. 'Sometimes I guess I feel bad because I get so mad at her when she's trying to be . . .'

The word stuck inside me.

'A parent, you mean?'

I nodded.

'I think we have discovered your next assignment,' Amy said. 'I'd like you to try to do something with your grandmother, in a grandmother-granddaughter kind of way. Go to a restaurant, go to a movie, play some games, go for a walk. You guys must have had a special relationship before, and it is different now, but it's important to spend some good time together to remember that relationship is still there, underneath, right?'

'I guess so.'

'Great. I'd like you to try that, then.'

'Okay,' I said. 'I'll try it. And if Gram doesn't feel like it . . .?'

'Maybe she can only be "parent" right now. But I think it would mean a lot to both of you to spend some fun time together. Okay?' She waited. 'So, I'll see you next week, then.'

'Sure.' I got up to leave.

'Aubrey?'

'Yeah?'

'Leave the M&M's jar, please.'

* * *

Fridays had got sort of boring now that Bridget's soccer team either practised or had a game, so I had spent the afternoon sitting on the porch with Martha, getting my homework out of the way. The leaves were changing and it was beautiful outside, but as everything turned golden in the setting sunlight I put my things away and went inside because it was so chilly. It was cold enough that I kept my fleece on inside the house.

I helped Gram set the table for dinner. She had made pot roast, which seemed just right for the weather. She brought the whole pot to the table and we sat down.

'School okay today?'

'Yeah, it was fine.'

'Hand in all your homework?'

'Yes.'

'Were you tired? You stayed up kind of late last night working on that – what was it?'

'My timeline.'

'Right, right. The timeline. It came out all right?'

'Yeah. Well, it looked better than some of them.' I thought of Marcus's timeline. He had skipped some of the dates on his poster and stuck them on with Post-its later.

'If you stay up late to work on your projects too often, we're going to have to set a bedtime, to make sure you aren't getting tired. You'll have to set aside a little more time in the afternoon to get your homework done.'

I wanted to tell her how good it made me feel to stay up late working, because then I slept a safe, dreamless sleep that lasted all the way until my alarm clock rang in the morning. I poked the veggies in my bowl.

'Hey, Gram?'

'Hey, Aubrey?'

'Do you think we could do something fun this weekend?'

'Fun? What did you have in mind?'

'You know, something that would be fun for us to do together.'

Gram wiped her mouth with her napkin and set her fork down to think.

'You know what you used to love, little girl?'

'What?'

'The Rolla Rink. You don't remember?'

'Only a little.'

'Oh, you used to love the Rolla Rink. Want to go there?'

Roller skating. Hot dog. But if it was something we used to like to do together, then maybe it was just the right thing.

Like bowling, we had to hand over our shoes at the counter. Rental skates cost two dollars a pair. The teenager at the counter stuffed our tennis shoes together into a little square cubby and gave us a number on a slip to pick them up again.

Gram and I walked in our socks to a bench to put on our skates. They were made of yellowing white leather with frayed red laces. I tied mine really tight and then stood up.

'Whoa!' I said, rolling away from the bench. I reached out to grab it, but Gram caught my hand instead.

'Stand up straight,' she said.

I straightened up and realized that the skates were not like ice skates or Rollerblades. I didn't have to worry about tipping over. I just had to worry about leaning forward or backwards.

Despite her directions, once Gram stood up, she rolled back towards the bench, catching herself just as she plunked back down. She let out a great laugh.

'Okay, I got it,' she said, getting to her feet again. We held hands as we approached the wooden floor inside the rink.

A pair of sisters skated together. I imagined Savannah skating round the edge of the rink.

I decided I had to do some pretending. *I am out with Gram, and Mom, Dad and Savannah are all back at her house.* Pushing the memories from my mind, I sent them to Gram's house so that I could meet them there later. *For now, I am out with my grandmother, like the old days.*

'We're going to have to let go,' Gram said. 'Or we'll pull each other down.'

I let go of her hand, leaning forward, lifting one foot and setting it down, then taking slow, gliding turns with each foot until I had circled the rink, avoiding the other skaters. My body remembered skating.

Gram's body was a different story. While it might have remembered skating, it seemed to be a little timid about doing it. As I came up behind her on my second loop, she had her arms out for balance and was moving slowly.

'I need to be careful,' she said. 'Or I am going to end up on my rear. On my bee-hind.'

'Try, it's okay,' I said. I looped the rink again. In the minute it took, a thought sped through my mind: if Gram got hurt, who would look after us?

By the time I got back to her, she had landed on her bee-hind. 'Ouch!' she cried.

I circled in front of her. She was laughing silently. 'Ooh, my!' she said when she'd had time to catch her breath. Tears of laughter gathered in the crickles of her eyes.

'Get up,' I said, tugging on her arms with both of my hands. Skaters around us were having to veer at the last second to miss us.

'You're going to fall too, pulling on me like that.'

I felt a bubble of laughter rising in my stomach and fell to my knees in front of her with a hard thump.

We were both laughing too hard to get up.

'Gram! We're in everyone's way!' I gasped as a boy and girl on either side of us clasped their hands together above our heads.

We crawled over to the wall of the rink and pulled ourselves up. Gram wiped her eyes with the backs of her hands.

'I'm a lot more steady now,' I said. 'It might be okay to hold hands.'

We took each other's hands again and stepped back into the rink.

After an hour of skating, I had beads of sweat on my forehead, my face hurt from smiling and my stomach ached from laughing. I was also hungry.

'There's a snack bar up front,' Gram said.

When we stepped off the rink, the regular floor felt funny. We stopped to take off our skates.

Gram ordered something I never would have expected: chilli-cheese fries and two really tall Sprites. We got a booth and sat for our snack.

The Rolla Rink insisted on playing oldies. Gram knew all of them and sang along.

'You know a lot of songs, Gram.'

'That I do. Did you know when I was younger, roller-skating was really cool? They used to have lots of places like this then. They had parties, like dances, for the kids. And at some diners the waitresses brought your food to your car on roller skates.'

'Why'd they stop that?'

'I guess people got hurt. The waitresses, I mean. As for the parties, I guess teenagers just became interested in other things.'

'How long do you want to stay?' I asked.

'Let's stay another hour or so after our snack.'

'Sounds good,' I said.

* * *

Two hours later, with very sore legs, we limped onto Gram's porch.

'You know, baby doll, I am going to be so stiff tomorrow,' Gram said. Then she chuckled. 'Let's do that again sometime!'

I held on to Gram's arm as we walked. I could tell that underneath her jacket sleeve, her skin was soft and a little saggy, and that under that, there was still strong muscle and bone.

The magic wore off when we got back in the house. The empty house. Gram shuffled to the answering machine. Even though the light wasn't blinking, she pushed the Play button anyway. The machine said, 'There are *no* new messages.'

Gram's face returned to its slack, worried look. Pretending had only worked for a little while. I felt the heaviness creeping back into my stomach and my heart.

'I'm going up to bed,' I said.

'Goodnight,' Gram said. She took the coffee pot and filled it with water.

Part of me wanted to offer to stay up with her, to hold her hand, to play cards, try to remember some jokes, but these things wouldn't have helped. So I turned and walked my body upstairs.

Dear Amy,

Is it okay if I write you a note?

I just wanted to say thanks, because I got my grandmother back for a few hours, and I realized how much I missed her.

I don't think that anything's different, but I guess trying was a good idea.

Love,

Aubrey

14

Gram made a super-good dinner. It was leftover meat loaf – meat loaf is better left over – on soft hamburger buns with ketchup, and veggie medley – that's peas, corn, carrots and green beans – and for dessert four different kinds of Jell-O – lime, blue raspberry, strawberry and orange – cut into cubes and served all together.

While I was still sitting at the table, stuffed, before we cleared the dishes, Gram said, 'Aubrey, I want to talk to you about something.'

I suddenly realized that only someone with something very important to say could find the time to make four kinds of Jell-O and cut it into cubes and serve it all together.

'I'm going to go on a trip,' Gram began. 'To visit your mother. Just for a couple of days.'

'Oh,' I said. 'Were you going to ask me to go?'

'I'm not sure what it will be like there. It's probably bet-ter if I go alone this time.'

'Fine. I'll be okay here by myself. Just get me some gro-ceries, and I can ride the bus to school, so stay as long as you like.' I decided to clear the table. Maybe that would be a sign of how fine I would be, on my own again.

Gram laughed. I turned and looked at her in surprise. 'Of course I'm not leaving you by yourself!' she exclaimed. 'No, no, Uncle David is going to come stay with you.'

'Is he bringing his family with him?' I asked. Uncle David was my favourite relative, but I didn't want the house all full up of company.

'No, just him,' Gram said. 'Sound okay?'

'Yeah,' I said. 'Sounds okay.'

On Saturday Uncle David's clunky car pulled into the driveway.

'Uncle David!' I called from the porch. I ran across the yard, meeting him halfway. He caught me in a hug, lifting me off the ground. When he set me down, he kept his arm round me as we walked to the porch. Gram stood there, waiting. She had her luggage with her. Gram hated flying, but she was going to take an aeroplane to Virginia. Two aeroplanes, actually, each way.

She hugged Uncle David extra tight. He kissed her cheek. Gram turned to me then. 'You be good, duckling,' she said. She hugged me for a long time. 'Carry my bags to the car for me?' I nodded and picked them up. She unlocked the trunk and I loaded the bags.

Gram stood in the open door of the car, lingering in the goodbye.

'Anything . . . anything you want me to tell your mother?' she asked.

'No,' I said.

Gram nodded and blew me one last kiss. Then she got in the car, started it and drove away.

Uncle David wanted to see my school. I hopped in the front seat of his car and told him which turns to take. He said it looked like a pretty nice school. He parked out by the basketball courts and told me to get the ball out of the back-seat. Then we played basketball for about an hour, until I was feeling a little sweaty and very thirsty.

Back at Gram's I poured us each a tall glass of juice from the fridge. Uncle David took his and drank standing up at the counter, but I sat down because my legs felt tired.

'It's good to see you,' he said.

'You too,' I replied.

'It's good for Gram to go to see your mother. For her, but also for your mother. She likes having visitors. It helps.'

Suddenly I felt very hot. Hotter than I had playing bas-ketball. 'How . . . how is she?'

Uncle David set his empty glass down on the counter.

'She's . . . good . . . Aubrey, let's go out. Let's go out and we can talk.'

I didn't know why it would matter where we were, but I shrugged and went to use the bathroom and get a jacket before we left.

We drove to a diner. I hadn't been out to eat in forever. I looked at the menu for a long time. It had a lot of things on it, even though nothing was too fancy. I didn't feel very hungry, but I ordered the turkey-on-toast hot dinner plate. It came with mashed potatoes and cranberry sauce. Uncle David ordered a Reuben sandwich with chips and a pickle.

After the waitress had taken our menus, I tore open a packet of sugar and poured it on the table. I drew swirly patterns in it with my pinky finger.

'So how is she?' I asked.

Uncle David raised his eyebrows at the sugar mess, but didn't say anything. He sat back, put his hands behind his head, then changed his mind and leaned forward. He watched me push the sugar around the table.

'She's doing okay.'

'Then why can't I see her? Why doesn't she call? You said she likes visitors. I could be a visitor.'

'Well, honey . . . she is still adjusting. She needs some time to heal. And so do you. If you saw her now, she might seem like the mom you lived with in the summer . . . We want you to see her when she is a little better, more like the mom you remember from before that.'

I took the salt shaker, tipping it upside down, and tapped a pile of salt onto the sugar swirls.

'Did she say anything about me? Is she mad at me?' I asked.

'Why would she be mad at you?' Uncle David asked.

I flattened my hands round the salt-and-sugar sea, pushing the grains into a steep mountain peak. I used my pinky to tap the mountain back down. Then I swept the whole pile into my hand and dumped it over the side of the table, onto the floor.

'You know,' I said, 'I heard her leave.'

'You did? Why didn't you tell someone?'

'I didn't know she was leaving leaving. It was in the morning, and I was in bed. The house was all quiet. It was always quiet in the morning, once it was just us. If Mom ever got up before me, I could hear her in the kitchen making coffee. Sometimes she dropped her mug on the floor and cried, and I had to go clean it up and help her. So I always listened.

'One morning I heard her walking around. That wasn't so weird. Then I heard the front door. I heard the car door. The car started, and she was gone.'

'Did you get up? Go after her?'

'No, I . . .' I closed my eyes to think. I covered them with my hands. The memory was so far away. 'I thought maybe it was okay. I thought she was just going out for a little bit. I was glad that she was doing something. I thought she was coming back.'

'So that morning . . .?'

'I went back to sleep. It was nice too. It was so quiet, and still, but not like when Mom was there. It was different. I felt alone and it felt good. When I woke up, it was almost lunchtime. She wasn't back, so I made some lunch and turned on the TV. I started to wonder if I should be worried.'

'Were you?'

I shook my head. 'I didn't want to be. So I just shut her out of my mind.'

'When she didn't come home that night . . .'

'That was scary. But I had to act like it didn't bother me. I had to. I was mad at her for being so . . . so . . .'

'It's okay. Tell me.'

'Well, she didn't seem to care if I was okay, so why should I worry about her? She was the one who left.'

Uncle David nodded.

'But there was this other part of me that really didn't want anyone else to be mad at her. I wanted people to leave us alone. They all kept saying they were sorry, but no one really knew what it was like.'

'I understand that, Aubrey.'

'Do you?'

'I think I do.'

'It wasn't right, was it?'

'Don't worry about that.' Uncle David relaxed his face just a little bit. His jaw and nose looked like Mom's. 'She didn't want to hurt you, either. Her doctor told me that she was so sad about what happened – and she was getting more and more sad, not less, as time passed – that her brain decided to pretend that nothing had happened. It couldn't pretend so easily at your house, where your dad and sister were missing, so she had to leave. If she was off on her own, maybe all three of you were okay together, somewhere else. She just couldn't feel any more pain – so her body took over, took her away from things. Made her get in the car, and just . . . drive . . . Her doctor says she can be okay again. She's already starting to come back.'

'What – what was she like?' I asked.

'What do you mean?'

'Growing up. What was she like?'

'Oh.' Uncle David thought for a minute. He squeezed the lemon in his water against the side of the glass with his straw, then stirred it. 'Lissie was just fine. Wonderful. She was sweet, loved to be the centre of attention, and usually got to be, being the youngest. But she shared it, you know. She wanted to be with you, or with someone at least, all the time.'

She sounded like Savannah. Maybe sometimes Savannah had reminded her of herself.

Uncle David opened his wallet and took out a photo of four children, himself and his sisters. He studied the photo, then handed it to me. My eyes settled on the widest smile, fixed on the face of the youngest.

'I know what you're looking for.' He sighed. 'I've been looking for it myself. Some hint from before that something was wrong.'

I nodded.

'It's not there,' he said.

'No,' I answered. 'I guess it isn't.'

The waitress brought our plates. We stared at them for a minute. Mine looked huge, with heaping globs of gravy, and the meat on Uncle David's sandwich was piled so thick I didn't know how he was going to fit his mouth round it.

'Let's eat,' he suggested.

I took my knife and fork and cut several bite-sized pieces, but didn't eat them. Uncle David noticed and put his sandwich back down. When he stopped chewing, he sipped his drink.

'She loves you,' he said. 'I know it's hard right now, but she does.'

I nodded and stuffed a bite into my mouth. Chewing was so hard. I sipped at my own soda, even though I hadn't swallowed yet.

Dear Jilly,

It was nice to see Gram when she came back. Even though she was only gone a few days, I missed her. I didn't even know it until she was back and I saw her again.

Gram says that Mom is okay. She is still very sad, and doesn't talk to anyone in the family about what happened, but she is talking to the doctor a lot. That seems to help her more than when she wasn't talking about things at all. Gram says everyone is trying hard and helping to make her better. Someone takes her out every day to spend some time outside and to do some errands and just to be with her so she doesn't feel alone. Aunt Linda got there before Gram left to stay with Mom for the next few weeks.

That's all I have to tell you.

Love,
Aubrey

15

My breath came in short gasps. The creases of my palms filled with sweat. I stood at the window, wishing away the weather.

'It's okay to wait,' Gram said. 'I'll drive you over when it stops.'

I'd ridden the school bus in the rain before, but it was a drizzly, soft and safe rain. This rain was pounding, sweeping, dizzying.

My hair was braided, in two tails, the same way Bridget would wear her hair, the way we'd planned.

I was going to see Amy today.

I had a science presentation. My report, 'The Understory Story: The Life Cycle of a Forest', was tucked in my backpack. It was six pages, plus the bibliography. Gram had marked the end of several days' work by buying me one of those clear plastic covers with a red plastic spine that slides on to hold the whole thing together.

'No,' I answered Gram. 'I-I'll get on the bus when it comes.'

'You're sure?' she asked.

'Yes,' I said.

The bus finally appeared and pulled to a sloshy stop.

'Bye, love,' Gram said, walking me to the door.

I ran outside, getting soaked. At the same time, Bridget sprinted towards the bus. No, towards me. When we met in the squishy grass, we stopped. I looked at Bridget's quickly soaking braids as she took my hand in hers.

'Thank you for your note,' Amy said. 'The one you left in my box last week.'

My toes squirmed in my tennis shoes. Wiggling my toes made my damp socks stick a little less.

'I was really glad to get it,' she added, unable to see my toes. 'It made me think about a few things. Do you mind if I share them with you?'

I shook my head.

'It made me wonder whether you keep a journal, or spend any time writing.'

'No.'

'Not at all?'

'Well, sometimes I write letters.'

'Who do you write to?'

'No one.'

'If you are writing letters, they are probably to someone.'

I felt embarrassment creep into my chest. Probably my cheeks were turning pink and showing it too. 'I write to Jilly.'

'Who is Jilly?'

'She's – was – she was Savannah's imaginary friend. We used to play with her, a long time ago.'

Amy didn't seem to think it was funny at all. 'Why do you write them?' she asked kindly.

I wondered if I could lift my toes individually. I couldn't. Just my big toes.

'Does it help you to write to her?'

I shrugged. 'Not really.'

'Why do you do it?'

'To do something.'

'Do you tell Jilly about how you're feeling?'

'Maybe a little.'

'Even if you don't tell her how you're feeling, does writing to her change how you're feeling?'

I stared out of the window. A bird twitched in the browning leaves in the bushes outside the office. It looked in two directions, then quickly flew away.

'Is it really Jilly you want to talk to?' Amy asked.

The sky was slowly becoming bluer as the rainy day drifted away. Grey clouds still hung in the sky, but they were lighter.

'No,' I whispered.

When I looked back at Amy, I saw that she was nodding and staring at me with searching eyes. Finally, she looked away and tapped her pen on her paper.

'I'm going to give you a tough assignment this time, Aubrey. I don't want you to do it this week, or this month, or even soon if you are not ready. Just sometime.'

'Sometime,' I repeated, to show I was listening.

'I want you to write to them. To the people you really want to talk to.'

To them.

Even though Amy's office was small, suddenly it seemed like she was sitting a million miles away. She was still talking, somehow. I closed my eyes to try to listen.

'I think it will be hard. But I think, in the end, it will help you. Those things we never say can stay with us forever. If we can find a way to say them, a little weight will be gone. I truly believe this will help you. I don't want to see what you write – you can just tell me if you do it, okay?'

I stared at her. I couldn't say anything.

I couldn't do it.

Amy held my gaze, as if to say *You can*.

She scribbled something on the paper. She handed it to me.

'This note is for you to go back to class. I'm giving you ten extra minutes, so you can walk slow, get some water, think, whatever you like. Please take your time.'

I nodded.

Amy picked up an orange envelope from her little

round table. She handed it to me. It said 'Aubrey' in perfect loopy black print.

'Your invitation. I'm having a Halloween party for my students. I would love for you to come. You can bring a friend. It'll be during lunch on Halloween.'

I nodded and stood up. Amy held out the M&M's jar. I shook my head and picked up my backpack.

Amy opened the door for me.

'You're doing really well,' Amy said. 'Please think about what we talked about, okay?'

Amy had been right about a lot of things. She had been right about sitting with people at lunch. She was right about doing my homework. She was right about spending time with Gram. But she couldn't be right about this.

'What's the matter with you?'

I was pouring my soda very slowly, listening to the fizzies spreading out in the plastic cup.

'What's the matter?'

'What?' I asked. I looked up to see Bridget staring at me from across the cafeteria table. 'Oh, nothing.'

'Well, guess what,' Bridget said, lowering her voice.

'What?' I asked, lowering mine.

'See that boy over there?'

'Bridget, there are hundreds of boys in here.'

'That one, in the blue stripes?'

'Oh, that one?'

'Don't look at him!'

'You asked me if I saw him! How am I supposed to see him without looking?'

'Sorry,' Bridget said. 'What do you think of him? Do you think he's cute?'

'What? I don't know.'

'Well, he is,' Bridget said. 'He's totally cute.'

'He is? Since when?'

'Since this morning.' Bridget had a dreamy look on her face. 'Christian Richards.'

I started laughing. 'You have a crush!'

Bridget lost the dreamy look and scowled at me. 'You shouldn't talk. You're the one who has a crush. On Marcus.'

'I do not!' I said. My eyes flitted over to where Marcus sat with a group of boys. I didn't have a crush on him. I couldn't explain it. Something about him drew my attention, but I didn't quite know what it was.

'Are you done with lunch?' Bridget asked quickly.

'What? No.'

'Look, Christian's heading to the trash. Let's go throw our stuff away. We can run into him,' Bridget said.

I rolled my eyes, but I shoved the rest of my lunch back into my paper bag and let her tug me out of my seat.

'Hi, Christian!' Bridget said when we got to the trash can.

'Hey,' Christian said. 'Are you guys coming to my Halloween party?'

'We're not sure yet,' Bridget said. 'Maybe we'll see you there?'

'Sure, see ya,' Christian said. He headed back to his table.

Bridget guided me out of the cafeteria towards the girls' room. 'He invited us to his Halloween party!'

'Everyone is invited. We got invitations in the mail. It's thrown by the class parents.'

'I kind of – did you want to go trick-or-treating?' Bridget asked.

I trick-or-treated with Savannah every year. This was going to be the year they let us go on our own, with me in charge, because I would finally be old enough.

I would never trick-or-treat again.

'No,' I said. 'Let's go to the party.'

It wasn't until I saw Amy in her costume that I realized I really didn't want to see her. I think she was supposed to be Little Bo Peep. She had a huge dress and a huge bonnet and a shepherd's crook.

I gave her a small wave and pinched Bridget's elbow to steer her towards the food table. I could have guessed there would be M&M's, and there were also dark chocolate cupcakes with orange frosting. There was a veggies-and-dip tray and turkey sandwiches on nice rolls that probably came from a bakery.

I took a celery stick and a carrot and put them on a

plate. Bridget gave me a funny look and put a turkey sandwich and a cupcake on my plate too.

The party was in a classroom near Amy's office. There were plenty of people there. Everyone had brought a friend, so only half the people there were Amy's kids. Once everyone was mixed up, you didn't really know who was who, though Marcus showed up without a friend. I watched him say hi to Amy. When he talked to her, his smile grew wider and even his eyes smiled. She gently touched his shoulder as she moved to say hi to another kid.

My eyes followed Marcus as he went to the food table. He looked different; it was something about his eyes.

Another kid walked up to Marcus and threw an M&M at him. Marcus laughed, put a candy in his left hand, and pinged it at the kid with his right thumb and middle finger.

But after the boy walked away, Marcus let his hair flop in front of him, and his smile went away.

I realized that Marcus was sad. Sometimes I forgot that I wasn't the only person in the world who could feel sad.

Bridget and I decided to go to Christian's Halloween party as cowgirls. I put on a jean skirt and a sleeveless white blouse, plus tights and a jean jacket, because Gram said I had to have them in the cold. We did our hair in braids and painted freckles on each other's cheeks. Bridget lent me a cowgirl hat and boots.

Bridget's mother drove us to the party. Most people were

already there when we arrived. The party was in the base-ment. The only lights were from flickering jack-o'-lanterns with battery lamps and strings of orange bulbs dangling from the ceiling. Christian and his mom were stringing up doughnuts. Christian's dad had set up a pumpkin-carving station on a mat on the floor. A lot of the boys were there flinging pumpkin guts at each other. I headed over to choose a pumpkin, but Bridget grabbed my hand and pulled me towards the doughnuts.

'Why are they hanging up doughnuts?' I whispered.

'It's a game,' Bridget explained. 'You can't use your hands and you have to eat the doughnut.' Then she raised her voice. 'Hi, Christian.'

'Hi, girls,' Christian's mother answered instead. 'Go ahead on the doughnuts.'

I approached a doughnut and got powdered sugar all over my nose as I ate it. Bridget laughed at me but obviously wasn't going to risk looking ridiculous in front of Christian.

'Come check out the coffin,' Christian said.

'What?' I asked.

Christian pointed towards the back of the room. There was one of those fake cardboard coffins where you reach in and feel the rotting corpse. It was probably just junk like spaghetti guts and peeled-grape eyeballs.

'I'll go,' Bridget said.

'You go ahead,' I told them. I didn't really want to check out a coffin.

I wandered over to the food table. Sitting on the wall side was Marcus, building a pyramid of candy corn.

'Hi, Marcus,' I said, sliding into the chair next to him and taking off my cowgirl hat.

I wasn't sure how to talk to him about what I wanted to. 'I saw you at Amy's today.'

'Yeah.'

'Does she help you?'

He shrugged. 'She's nice.'

'Yeah,' I said. 'Why do you see her?'

'Family stuff,' he said.

'Oh,' I said. 'Me too.'

I was ready to leave it there, but Marcus kept talking.

'My dad left. He left last year.'

'I'm really sorry,' I said.

'My dad left because I was bad.'

'No, Marcus, that's not why.'

'It was. I could never sit still. I was never quiet. I wouldn't eat my dinner. That's what he used to say to me. "Sit still!" "Be quiet!" "Eat your dinner!"'

I don't know what made me do it. It was probably only okay because it was kind of dark at the party, and our hands were hidden behind the black crêpe-paper tablecloth. I took Marcus's hand and held it. It was sticky and hot, but I held it anyway. Marcus looked surprised.

'It wasn't your fault,' I said.

Marcus shook his head. He did it for a few minutes, his hair flopping into his face. He shook his head like he was trying to shake memories right out of his ears.

* * *

The next day at lunch, before I found Bridget, I spotted Marcus sitting alone and picking at his school lunch. I sat down across from him.

'Hi,' I said.

'Hi,' he said without looking up.

'Listen,' I said. 'I want to tell you something.'

He looked up and shrugged. I guess he meant I could go ahead.

'My mom left too. I mean, like your dad did. I should have told you last night.'

Marcus nodded and went back to stirring his veggie medley. Carrots, corn, green beans, butter beans.

'Did she leave because of you?' he asked.

I thought very carefully for a few minutes.

'She didn't stay because of me,' I said.

I could tell that under the table, Marcus was starting to tap his foot. Above the table, he nodded, letting his hair fall into his eyes. I stood up to leave. As I walked away, even though there had been a table between us, I felt like Marcus had given me a hug.

~~Mom —~~

~~Dear Mama,~~
   ~~What's Colorado like? I've never been there.~~
   ~~Well, you know that. You know all the places~~
~~I have been.~~
   ~~Why~~

~~Hi Mom,~~
   ~~I wish that~~

~~Hi Dad,~~
   ~~I really, really miss you, and I wish you were~~
~~here~~

16

I sat on the couch, doing my homework with the TV on. My binder was open in my lap. My feet rested on the coffee table, my math book balancing on my knees. Gram came in and stood behind me and put her hands on either side of my head.

'I want to talk to you about Thanksgiving,' she said.

Holidays. *Not listening, not listening. Not. Listening.* I kept my eyes on the TV screen, then lowered them to copy the next equation out of the book.

'Aubrey.' She pressed on my head a little, to make me listen. 'We got invitations from your aunts and uncles, who all dearly want you to come. And we got another invite that I thought you might like better, so I said yes to that.'

My heart fluttered. Had she called again? Would we see her for Thanksgiving?

'We're going next door,' Gram finished.

Next door . . . to Bridget's.

I tried to push aside the hurt that Mom hadn't called and tried to be with me for Thanksgiving. Of course I would love to be with Bridget for the holiday. It was nice of Gram to think of that instead of having us go off to relatives' houses.

'What's Mom doing?' I asked.

'Uncle David is going to be with her up until Thanksgiving, and then he is going home to be with his own family. Your mom said she didn't want to be with family on the holiday just yet. She is going to be with some older women from church who have Thanksgiving together.'

'That sounds good,' I said. 'Bridget's, I mean. That's what I want to do.'

'We can call your mom, you know. To say happy Thanksgiving.'

I shook my head.

'It's all right,' Gram said. 'You don't have to.' Then she leaned over and kissed the top of my head.

'There's the list of food for Thanksgiving. Let me know if there's anything else you want. I'm bringing the things with stars.'

I scanned the list: Turkey, stuffing, gravy, rolls, *mashed potatoes, *corn, *cranberry sauce . . .

It all seemed pretty standard, but I thought hard. Something was missing.

'Where are the sweet potatoes?'

'Oh. You like sweet potatoes? That's easy, I'll pick up a few, throw them in the oven and bake them.'

'No, not like that. It's like a dish, you know, with marsh-mallows.'

'I don't know, honey. Do you know what it's called?'

'Sweet potato . . . no. I don't know. Dad . . . Dad always made it.'

That was the part I remembered. He loved that dish, would cook it himself, always, and talk about it all day, make Savannah and me come and smell it when he took it out of the oven. I'd watch him sneak a taste before it was time to eat, smooth out the missing bite so Mom wouldn't know. It was so sticky sweet that I didn't even always like it, but now that was all I wanted for Thanksgiving.

'Do you know what was in it? Besides the marshmallows?'

'I-I think I might.'

'Can you tell me, and maybe I could look up the recipe?'

'No, no that's all right. I-I'll do it.'

Gram looked at me softly.

'I'll get you the sweet potatoes and the marshmallows, then. You can take care of it.'

'Savannah, the parade's on!'

'Ooh! The parade!'

Savannah runs into the living room, holding Bunny, her limp stuffed rabbit. She crashes into me as she sits down, facing the TV, eyes eager.

'Girls! Do you smell this? All this wonderful food?' Dad calls from the kitchen.

'No!' I call back.

'Yes!' calls Savannah.

'Just kidding, I can!' I say. I get up, dropping my own stuffed giraffe, and head to the kitchen.

Mom strains the turkey juice for the gravy. She smiles at me. When she finishes, she wipes her hands on her apron and announces that she is heading to the bathroom. When she leaves the room, Dad waves me over to the stove. He finds a big spoon and gets me a steaming taste of everything that is cooking, blowing on each spoonful and holding one hand under it as he passes it to me. I am chewing on only slightly softened carrots when Mom comes back.

'What are you doing?' she asks.

'Nothing,' Dad says. 'Just getting ready to mash the sweet potatoes. Aubrey, can you get me the brown sugar?'

I drag a chair to the counter, climb up and open the cabinet . . .

'How's it going?' Gram entered the kitchen, peering into my mixing bowls with a look that hinted at suspicion.

'Fine,' I answered, stirring some more.

'You look like something went wrong,' she said.

'No, I'm just . . . trying to remember.'

'I see,' Gram said.

I closed my eyes again.

'Aubrey, get me the nutmeg.'

'Gram, do we have nutmeg?'

When we got to Bridget's at five o'clock, I was holding my sweet potatoes in two hands with pot holders. Gram had brought over the mashed potatoes and was going back for the corn. The can of cranberry sauce was in the deep pocket of my winter coat.

'They're here!' Bridget cried, flinging the door open. She must have been watching for us out of the window.

'She's been waiting for you all day,' her father explained, stepping behind her and opening the door a little wider. 'She's always wanted to have a friend over on a holiday.'

That was something I had always wanted too, but I couldn't say that, not when it felt so strange and lonely, this first holiday without my family. Watching Bridget's dad pull her gently backwards by her ponytail to make room for us to come through the door made me miss Dad again.

'These are the sweet potatoes. My dad used to make them like this,' I said stiffly, holding them out to him. I wanted him to understand. Maybe he did, because he nodded and smiled at me as he took the casserole.

'Aubrey made them herself,' Gram said. 'Here, take my dish too. I'll run back and get the last thing.'

Gram left me there, alone. No, I wasn't alone, of course not. Bridget must have been instructed in being a hostess, because she pulled on the sleeve of my coat to help me out of it and put it in the coat closet. I had never put my coat there before on all my visits to her house.

The turkey was already on the table, and there were plates set. Bridget's dad put our dishes on empty spots in the middle of the table. Danny was already in his high chair, gnawing on a soft roll. Mabel skipped in, offering me a hat like one on her own head: a brown construction-paper circle with construction-paper feathers.

'We made them at school!' she said excitedly. 'This one is for you!'

'Thank you,' I said, taking the hat and slipping it onto my head. It was too tight, and my stomach jumped a little as my fingers passed over my scar. 'Oh! Bridget, there's a can in my coat.'

She looked at me. It had been an odd thing to say, I realized. 'The cranberry sauce.'

'Oh!' Bridget ran off to get it. She insisted on opening it herself. She splunked it into a bowl and brought it to the table in one wobbly cylinder.

Bridget's mother appeared in the kitchen. 'Hello, Aubrey,' she said, touching my shoulder and giving me a kiss on the cheek. 'Happy Thanksgiving. Pick a spot; have a seat.'

Everyone was gathering at the table. Gram was back even before I sat down. She sat on one side of me, and Bridget on the other. Mabel sat next to Bridget. Danny's high chair was pushed close to his parents' seats.

'Do you have anything you do as a tradition before dinner?' Bridget's mom asked me kindly.

'Take the bread, sweetie,' Mom says, tearing a piece off a round loaf. 'Pass it to your sister and help her tear some.' I hold out the loaf to Savannah, and she grips a small piece in her fist and we both pull . . .

'No,' I said, but I felt like I was choking.

'At our house we like to go round the table and say what we are thankful for. Does that sound all right?'

'Fine,' I whispered.

'I'll go,' Bridget's dad volunteered. 'I'm thankful that we are all able to sit and share this wonderful meal together.'

I didn't listen as Bridget's mother shared hers, and Danny didn't get a turn, obviously. Mabel chirped that she was thankful for Mommy and Daddy and kitties and puppies, though two of those things she didn't have.

'I'm thankful that a new friend moved in,' Bridget said, smiling at me with a little embarrassment.

It was my turn. There was nothing I could say. I was thankful, I really was, to be included in this nice family on their holiday, that they thought of inviting me to make things easier. I was thankful that Gram had found me, that she helped me. But I couldn't say any of this, because it would mean I was forgetting where I really should be, who my real family was.

I took Bridget's hand, the one next to me, and reached for Gram's. Both of them squeezed back. I looked around the table, seeing Bridget's parents gazing at me, tears gathering in the corners of her mother's eyes.

'I am thankful' – Gram interrupted the heavy silence I had caused – 'for my granddaughter, whose life is as much a gift to me today as the day she was born.'

Bridget's dad broke the next pause a moment later. 'Let's say grace.' He took his wife's hand and Danny's small one. Soon we were all linked round the table. As he recited the prayer, I looked at all of them, their heads lowered ever so slightly, except for Mabel's. She looked right at me, and I was glad that I did have some family to be with, even if I missed mine.

Daddy,

I miss you the most, you know. It's strange to say that, because I don't really think that way. I don't think of you more than them. But I always thought of our family you&me and Savannah&Mom. With you two gone, Mom is still closer to Savannah. Or, I mean, she wants to be. She won't have me. She doesn't want me the way you always did.

I'm not mad at you, because there's a difference between choosing to leave and not choosing to leave. You didn't choose to leave. Maybe Mom did. I don't know what she was thinking, but she could have chosen to come back since then and she hasn't.

I want to tell you about that, what happened with Mom. And I want to tell you about being with Gram and about school and about how writing to you was Amy's idea and how it took me a long time to do it.

I want to tell you about how I made the sweet potatoes for Thanksgiving and I made them just right. And I want to tell you about how everyone liked them even though they had never eaten them before — even baby Danny ate them. You don't know him. He's Bridget's little brother. You don't know Bridget, either. She's my best friend.

Anyway, the sweet potatoes got passed around the table again and again, until they were all gone. It made me happy because it was like you came to dinner too, in a way.

Maybe you know all this already, or maybe you are reading this letter over my shoulder. That makes me feel good, to think that. Or maybe when I seal it and take it outside and let it go, then you will know what it says.

This is what I want you to know: that I love you. I miss you. I hope even though I'm growing you would still recognize me if you saw me. I will always be your Aubrey. You will always be the best dad. I wish you hadn't had to go.

Goodbye for now,

Love,
Aubrey

17

I woke up to find the brown, cold, frozen world still cold and frozen but soft white.

'Gram!' I yelled. I abandoned the window in my room and raced downstairs barefoot.

Gram stood at the kitchen stove, apparently unexcited. The radio was on. 'I know about the snow already. School's cancelled. It's supposed to keep up like this all day.'

That was awesome news.

'What are you cooking?' I asked.

'Pancakes. You're going to need a good breakfast.'

'Why? There's no school.'

'You'll be playing outside all day. You'll see.'

After feeding me a pile of pancakes, Gram helped me bundle up from head to toe. She dug a partially deflated snow tube out of the back closet. We took turns adding air to it. Then she shoved me out the back door.

Like I remembered from visiting Gram in the winter before, Vermont's snow was deeper, drier, and thicker than Virginia's. True to the forecast, the snow was still coming down. I clumped through the heaps in the backyard for maybe five minutes before the back door opened at Bridget's and she came out, all ready to go sledding too.

'Oh good, you're out here. My whole family is coming!' she said. 'There's a great sledding hill across the street. Come on.'

We trooped to the hill and took a few trudgy rides down.

'It's not working so well,' I said.

'Dad will come out soon. He can push us and it'll be really good.'

We climbed back up and waited. Not too much later her family came out, Mabel skipping along, holding tight to her dad's arm so that she could jump through the snow heaps while he carried her snow tube. Bridget's mom held a pudgy, bundled Danny, whose nose was already turning pink.

'Push us, Daddy,' Bridget demanded.

'Is that how you ask for things?' he asked.

'Please!' we both cried.

'You got it,' he said. Bridget sat on her snow tube first, holding the handles. Her dad put his hands over hers and started to run behind her. When she was going very fast, he let go, and she whooshed down the hill, screaming happily.

I was next. He ran behind me, and when he let go I

was flying, holding tight to the handles. My heart, too, picked up speed. At the bottom of the hill I crashed into Bridget. We laughed. A minute later a zooming Mabel toppled into us. When she stopped moving, her eyes were big and terrified.

'AGAIN!' she screamed.

Bridget and I tugged her out of the snow. Each of us pulling on one of her mittened hands, we hurried back up the hill.

The track became packed down and slick, making us sled faster. Flying down the hill, I was actually happy. I grew more and more excited with each run. I wasn't just heading down the hill. I was heading towards Christmas. Christmas, the time of family and wishes coming true. It was the time Gram said we came back to her after Grandpa died, and things got better. If Mom was waiting for the right time, Christmas was it. It had to be. I was heading towards my mother.

Gram told me the whole family would be coming for Christmas this year, meaning all my aunts and uncles and cousins.

'Do I need to move out of my room?' I asked. 'Aunt Melissa and Uncle Steve used to stay there.'

'No, I want you to have your room. You might want a private place to go. We'll figure something else out for them.'

Of course, there was the room where my parents had usually stayed, but she didn't say that out loud.

'What about Mom?' I asked.

'Your mom is going to go down to Georgia to be with your dad's family.' When I made a face, Gram added, 'They wanted her to know she's still their family too.'

I heard Gram, but I didn't believe her. It was important for Mom to show me she was still *my* family, not anyone else's. Whatever Gram thought the arrangements were, Mom would come here. She had to.

I usually wasn't that interested in clothes or looking too neat, but the Friday before Christmas I really wanted to look just right as our family started to arrive. When I got off the bus, I went straight inside and washed my hair, and then I blow-dried it so that it was pretty smooth. It took a long time because I'd never done it before. Then I tied it back with a black ribbon. Gram had bought me a new red dress for Christmas, so I put that on with my black dress-up shoes.

Before going downstairs, I stopped in front of the mirror. Mom would certainly see how much I had grown when she got here.

'That dress is for Christmas Eve Mass,' said Gram when she saw me.

'I want to wear it now,' I said. For goodness' sake, Gram could have just said I looked nice.

Gram had been cooking all day. She wanted to have some things ready for the next few days to make it easier.

I looked into a casserole dish with green, yellow and grey goop.

'What's that?' I asked.

'Spinach artichoke dip,' Gram said. 'You won't like it.'

The doorbell rang. I couldn't get to the door fast enough. I pulled it open.

It wasn't her.

It was Uncle David, Aunt Katherine and their kids, Madison and Todd.

I felt the smile leave my face.

'Merry Christmas, Aubrey,' Aunt Katherine said.

'Merry Christmas,' I echoed. 'Come in.'

Aunt Katherine stepped through the door and gave me a soft, lovely hug. Uncle David took a turn to squeeze me too, and said, 'You're dressed up.'

'I wanted to look nice for you,' I said.

Uncle David's eyes searched mine. I looked away.

Madison and Todd stared at me like I had a disease. They didn't hug me or say Merry Christmas. I tried to remember their ages. Fourteen and twelve?

Gram came to the door, and there was a lot more hugging and holiday wishes. Then she saw me standing to the side. She must have sensed my about-to-get-a-stomach-ache mood, because she said, 'Aubrey, help me bring all the snacks into the living room, now people are getting here.'

It was Gram's usual trick of keeping me busy. I went to the kitchen and started moving snacks.

The next time the doorbell rang it was Aunt Melissa and Uncle Steve and my cousin Chloe, who was just four. There was a repeat of hugging. I peered around them on the porch, but there was no one else there.

'All right, Aubrey?' Uncle Steve asked.

'Oh yeah,' I answered, shutting the door slowly. I only noticed then how much cold air it had let in.

Everyone else came to greet them, and there were even more hugs. The hugs were slow and heavy, not light and jolly. Everyone was thinking of those who were not here.

As if forgetting, Madison rushed in and picked up Chloe and spun her round. Chloe laughed.

I tried to read the smiles on the grown-ups' faces, to see if they were really happy or if the smiles were hiding sadness. Even though it was crowded in the front hall and my elbow was nearly linked to Uncle Steve's, I felt ten miles away from everyone. There was an invisible wall between us.

I sneaked the door open again and looked out.

She still wasn't here.

I am in Gram's kitchen. I am small. I stand between two tall legs, clenching the fabric of their jeans in my fists. I peek between the knees of the jeans and giggle. Uncle David wears a Santa hat and hides on the other side of the legs. When I peek out again, he makes a face and I laugh.

The legs are Mom's. She reaches round and picks me up. She hands me a cup of juice from the counter and I drink it, starting to feel sleepy. She makes a sling with her arms, turning me so that I lie like a baby. She talks to everyone, Gram, Daddy, Uncle David, Aunt Katherine; Madison clatters by with a noisy toy. Mom carries me to the living room, and we sit on the couch next to the twinkling Christmas tree, but I keep my eyes shut and begin to dream . . .

Aunt Linda, Uncle Douglas and my teen-aged cousins Max, Andrew and Sarah came next, but she didn't come.

We ate all the snacks, and she didn't come.

Aunt Katherine passed around school photos of Madison and Todd, and she didn't come.

We ate dinner, and she still didn't come.

Aunt Melissa brought around the dessert, pecan pie, and stopped at my place.

'I don't want any,' I said. My head was on the table, and the ribbon had long since come loose and let out strands of hair. 'Actually, excuse me for a minute, please.'

I went upstairs to my room.

Why wasn't she here yet?

I left the lights off and sat at my desk. I put my head down again.

Well, Christmas was still a few days off. She could still make it.

Yes, that was it. Such a Christmas surprise would only take place on true Christmas. Maybe Christmas Eve. I would just have to wait a little longer. Besides, if she did come tonight, I wouldn't want her to see me sad. I would want her to see how well I was doing, how we could be happy together because I was learning how to be happy again. How I wouldn't bother her at all or be hard to take care of.

I trooped back downstairs, little bursts of determination guiding my steps.

Andrew, Madison and Todd had started a game of Scrabble on the coffee table in the living room.

'Can I play?' I asked.

Todd and Andrew kept quiet, but Madison said, 'Sure,' and tossed the bag of letters at me.

I thought as a rule up north there had to be snow on Christmas. But there wasn't. After that first snow had melted, the world was just brown again.

On Saturday night we went out to get a tree. And I don't mean we drove to some parking lot. We bundled up, went out in the woods and looked for one. Aunt Melissa seemed most convinced that she knew what kind of tree we wanted, so she made the final decision, and Uncle David and Uncle Steve used a little hatchet and a saw to cut the tree down.

It was one of three little firs in a row. As our Christmas tree came down, I wondered if the other little firs would miss him.

We dragged the tree back to the house, and a big show of standing it upright began in the living room. It seemed a lot bigger, now that it was inside. I thought of the little out-door firs.

The ornament boxes had been brought down from the attic and waited in the hallway. No one was looking at the decorations as they helped set up the tree or made hot chocolate in the kitchen to warm everyone up. So I opened the boxes myself, gathered a few bright round ornaments into my hands, and snuck out the front door.

Going off into the woods by myself at night was not something I'd say is a good idea, but I wasn't going too far, and I remembered the way. After a few minutes I came to the fresh stump and the two remaining firs. I set the ornaments on the ground, trusting the moonlight to help me find them again. I squatted next to the stump, reaching out to touch the fresh-cut wood. Something sticky got on my fingers. A glistening purple syrup. Sap.

I collected the decorations and started hanging them on the two trees.

'Hey!' a voice called.

I turned. 'Hey, Bridget,' I said.

'What are you doing?' she asked.

'Decorating,' I said.

Bridget wore an expression almost like a mother as she said, 'Where are your gloves? You'll get frostbite!'

I hung up the last ornament, got my mittens out of my pocket and put them on. Bridget's expression went back to normal.

'I was coming over to say Merry Christmas before we go away,' Bridget said. She was going to her cousins' for Christmas. 'But I saw you leave the house. I called you, but you didn't hear me, so I followed you.'

'I didn't know,' I said.

'Well, I brought you a present. Merry Christmas.' She held out a package. I took it from her. She must have wrapped it herself, because the red and gold paper was folded unevenly.

'Oh, thank you. I didn't get you anything yet,' I admitted. 'I didn't go shopping yet.'

'That's okay. Mom took me to get that. It's just a book. You can open it later.' Bridget turned to look at the trees. 'They look pretty, with the decorations.'

'We should go back,' I said. 'Before people freak out.'

'Yeah, I'm not supposed to be out in the woods at night,' Bridget said. She paused, then asked, 'You *are* okay, Aubrey, right?'

I started to walk and she came along beside me.

'You mean about Christmas?'

'Mom said Christmas might make you more sad than happy this year, and it was hard for me to be happy, thinking you were sad.'

'You can go ahead and be happy. I'm going to be happy, when . . .'

'When what?'

'Nothing, never mind.'

The thing about wishes is that you can't tell them to anyone, or they don't come true.

We were back at our yards.

'Well, Merry Christmas, Aubrey,' Bridget said, giving me a hug.

'Merry Christmas.'

On Christmas Eve morning we had blueberry muffins and hot chocolate for breakfast. Christmas Eve always seems like the longest day of the year. I played board games and watched movies with my cousins, but I kept looking out of the window. I wanted it to snow. If it snowed, it would be a sign that Christmas magic was working as it should be.

For dinner Gram made a feast of beef tenderloin, peas and mashed potatoes.

Then it was time to get ready for church, so I put my red dress on. Aunt Katherine was helping Madison and Sarah do their hair up in curls, so she did my hair too, with a hot curling iron. She piled the curls loosely with pins and threaded the black ribbon through so that it went round the outside almost like a headband.

'You look enchanting,' she said. 'Scoot and finish getting ready.'

I got my nice coat and my thin black gloves. It really did feel good, being all pretty. I didn't know how I was going to sit through Mass, knowing that when I got back Mom might be here.

It took three cars to get us there. The service was so boring. I read on the programme that this Mass is also called a vigil – the Solemn Vigil of Christmas.

'What's a vigil?' I whispered to Gram. A nice thing about Gram is that she thinks it's okay for kids to ask questions in church.

She whispered back, 'A vigil is when you stay awake watching. It's supposed to mean that we're staying up all night waiting for Jesus.'

I guess I got the idea of a vigil, but it wasn't like Jesus was going to show up in the flesh.

When we got back to Gram's house, I couldn't tell if there was an extra car because there were so many, but our old car definitely wasn't there. Maybe she had come in a different one. I flew to the porch before everyone, flung open the door and rushed inside. Out of breath, I searched every room downstairs, but she wasn't there.

My heart pounded as I stood near the door and caught my breath.

'What's the matter, dear?' Aunt Melissa asked, coming in with a sleeping Chloe on her shoulder.

'Nothing. Um, goodnight, Aunt Melissa. Merry Christmas. I'm going up to bed.'

The walk up the stairs was long and slow. There was still tomorrow. She would come tomorrow. She had to.

* * *

'Aubrey, honey, let Savannah go first. She's so excited and she's been waiting.'

I've been waiting too, though. Look at the pile of presents spilling out from under the tree! I've waited for everyone to get up, for Mom to make the coffee, for Savannah and me to shovel down bowls of cereal we didn't even want. It seems like I'll never get into those presents.

'It's Christmas. Wake up, sweetheart.' Gram shook me gently.

'Oh,' I said. 'Oh!'

I pushed the covers to the floor and jumped out of bed. I ran downstairs.

My eyes scanned the relatives, who were all drinking coffee and eating crumb cake. She still wasn't here.

Gram rushed after me with a bathrobe and socks. 'It's colder than you think this morning,' she said as I pulled them on.

'Sweetie, come sit by me,' Aunt Melissa said. I sat on the arm of the couch next to her. She pulled my hair out from the collar of the bathrobe where it had got stuck.

'Have some of my cake,' she said, holding the plate up to me. I broke off the tiniest bit and ate it.

A hall table had been pushed against the wall opposite the tree. On it were three framed photographs – Savannah, Dad and Mom. Two candles had been put next to Dad's and Savannah's pictures. The table had collected a few cards and small presents.

I looked at it and willed myself not to feel anything.

Throughout the morning things were handed to me, and I did whatever the hands seemed to suggest I do next. I opened presents. I ate cake. I drank hot chocolate. I returned hugs and cheek-kisses.

Whenever I had a chance, I went to the window and looked out. I went to the door and opened it. Where was she?

Uncle David noticed me at the window again. 'Sport,' he called to me. When I didn't turn from the window, he tried again. 'Aubrey. Come sit by me.'

I joined him on the sofa. I curled my legs up and rested my head on his chest.

'Christmas can be tiring,' he said. 'And we were out late. Just rest for a little.'

I tried to keep my eyes open, to wait, but he was right, it was hard. I was tired.

Aunt Katherine woke me at four o'clock for Christmas dinner. I shook my head, and she left me on the couch, where I was. I kept my eyes and ears open, watching, listening. From the dining room came the sounds of dishes, silverware and glasses, sometimes brief laughter. They kept the lights dim, and before the meal was over, the sun had set. Christmas was ending.

The phone. Maybe she would call to say Merry

Christmas. Maybe that was it. Maybe I'd been waiting the wrong way.

I went to the empty kitchen. I pulled a chair over to the counter by the phone and put my head down to wait.

Aunt Katherine found me again. She had a plate ready for me, ham and something and something. I didn't look too closely. 'You should try to eat,' she said kindly.

I didn't respond, and she went back to the dining room.

Gram came to the kitchen and pulled up a chair so that she was facing me. She looked at me so carefully; then she got up again, went to a cabinet. Opened her address book. Took a piece of paper from it. She handed it to me. A phone number.

'There. Call her.'

'No.'

'You want to talk to her.'

'No.'

'Aubrey –'

'No!' I yelled. 'That's not how it's supposed to be!'

Gram sighed. 'Tell me, how is it supposed to be?'

'She's supposed to come see me! Or she's supposed to at least call to wish me Merry Christmas!'

'We didn't call her, either,' Gram said. 'Sweetheart, time and space. If she isn't here, she isn't ready to come yet. If she isn't calling, she isn't ready to talk yet. I'm really sorry. If you want to try, please try, the number is right here.'

But I didn't want to try. I didn't want to have to try. She was the parent. It was her job to try.

'I hate her,' I said. I left the kitchen.

Christmas was over.

Dear Baby Jesus,

I know I haven't talked to you in a really long time. Not even at church on your birthday.

I don't know why you took my family away from me. I don't know why you know where my mother is and don't send her back to me. I wish things could be different than they are but I don't know how to make them different. I don't think it's my job. I think that's the grown-ups' job and maybe you should tell them to get going.

Anyway, I'm going to forget it. If my mom doesn't want to see me, or even talk to me on Christmas, then I don't want to see her or talk to her ever again. Keep her safe, wherever she is, but tell her to forget me. It's the best thing for everybody.

Oh, and happy birthday.

Love,
Aubrey

18

Frost laced the edges of my window. Even though I could feel the cold seeping in, I pressed my palm against the glass, watching a foggy outline of my hand appear. With my fingernails I scratched ALP – Aubrey Lynne Priestly – in the corner of the glass, letting the falling frost collect on the windowsill.

Gram had pulled some extra blankets from the trunk in the attic, so I climbed back into bed under the colourful layers of afghans and quilts. I found my mittens on the nightstand and put them on, and tugged a fleece cap over my head.

When Gram came in to announce it was nearly noon and I should get up, she laughed. Then she sat on the bed and said, 'Sometimes I forget my Aubrey is a southern belle.'

'What do you mean?' I asked grumpily, pulling off the mittens and hat.

'This kind of winter is new for you,' she said. 'Did you know the heat's on full blast?'

I shook my head and smoothed down my staticky hair.

Gram traced her fingers along the stitching on the top quilt, letting quiet settle in the room.

'Gram?'

'Hmm?'

'Did you make resolutions this year?'

She continued tracing and seemed to think. Then she said, 'No.'

I thought she must be lying, because she waited too long to answer. If she really didn't have any, she would have said so right away. 'Me neither,' I agreed.

I was lying too.

Deciding not to think about Mom was easier than I thought.

On Monday I didn't think of her on the school bus while Bridget chattered away next to me.

On Tuesday I didn't think of her in language arts, where I took lots of notes with new, bright-coloured gel pens I'd got in my Christmas stocking.

On Wednesday I didn't think of her at lunch, when Bridget kept track of every move of Christian Richards.

But at night, when everything slowed down, and the

house was dark, and the only sounds were the radiators ticking and Martha padding from one empty bed to the next, a lump grew in my throat. My eyes swelled with water, even though they were shut.

Bridget was having a sleepy day. That's what her mom called it, anyway, to explain why Bridget didn't come to the door to let me in.

'She's on the couch. If you don't see her, she's hiding under that old blanket. She's got movies on.'

I headed through the kitchen to the living room, where a cartoon movie was playing. I sat down on top of the blanket mound.

'What's up?' I asked.

'Ehh,' Bridget responded. She pulled the blanket off her face. 'Hi, Aubrey.'

'Hi,' I said. 'Can I watch?'

Bridget nodded and scooted over a little.

'Are you sick?' I asked.

'No,' she said. 'I just feel like lying around.'

'Okay,' I said. That made sense to me.

So we lay around on the couch, and then we lay around on the floor and drew lazy pictures with crayons, and then we lay around on the couch again.

Bridget's mom came in and was surprised that we were still lying there.

'Sweetie, what's the matter today?' she asked Bridget.

'Humph,' said Bridget. 'Nothing.'

'Mommy, c'mere,' Mabel called from the kitchen.

'In a minute,' she yelled back. 'Bridgie, let me see if you have a temperature.' Bridget let her mother feel her face. 'I don't think you feel hot,' she said.

'Mommy!' Mabel called.

Her mother said to Bridget, 'Do you have any sniffles?'

My stomach started to hurt. Maybe I was the one who didn't feel good.

I stood up. 'Let's play a game or something, Bridget. Something really long and good.'

Bridget nodded, and her mother left, calling to Mabel, 'Here I come!'

We got out Monopoly. We read the directions and counted all the pieces and got out a calculator for just in case. I decided to be the banker and Bridget would give out the property cards. We played and played and I thought of nothing but Monopoly, of the little doggie I was moving around the board, and the hotels I built on the yellow properties. In the end, I won.

I dreamed I could hear her. She was talking to me . . . no . . . about me. But who was she talking to? Dad?

The clock on my nightstand said 10:15. The numbers seemed too clear for dreaming . . . 10:16. 10:17. And I could still hear her.

'I need to see her,' she was saying.

Me. She needed to see me.

Someone else was talking, faintly, but getting louder.

'No. Not tonight. You are not waking her up.'

That was Gram, her voice angry. I could feel it filling the house and shaking me.

It wasn't a dream at all.

I threw off the covers and ran to the top of the stairs. I stood there, listening, my heart pounding.

My mother was downstairs.

'Mama,' I whispered. But my feet were glued, glued to the old, cracked floorboards of Gram's house.

'I'm her mother. I need to see her.' She was pleading now.

'You can't take time off from your child and just pick right up! Aubrey has finally got some stability back in her life. You can wait until tomorrow to see her, and then she is going to school.'

Mom didn't say anything.

Gram slammed something down. 'You left her!' she yelled.

'I know.' Mom's voice sounded as if she was choking. 'But I didn't know then. I didn't know. I wasn't thinking. I don't remember it.'

My breath stopped.

I had been forgotten. But she didn't leave me behind on purpose. She didn't know.

I heard Gram starting to talk again, still angry, but I couldn't understand what she was saying, just the harsh tones.

Gram, stop being so mad at her; you don't understand.

'Mama,' I gasped. She would never hear me, my voice was scrunched up so small.

'Let me see her!' Mom was nearly screaming now. 'You can't keep her from me!'

But Gram was the one who took care of me. She was the one who remembered me, who found me, who every day made sure I was okay. Mom shouldn't yell at her, either.

But she was here now. She had come back for me.

That must mean something.

My feet became unglued.

'I'm coming!' I put in the strength to shout, but the words floated away, teeny-tiny, as I hurried down the stairs.

I stood in the kitchen doorway, blinking in the light.

Gram looked livid when she saw me. Her face was bright red and her eyes were glistening and her mouth was clamped shut tight.

But Mom crossed the room.

She also had a red face and wet eyes. Her skin looked tired and stretched too tight, when it used to look creamy soft and gently smooth, and her dark hair, which had always been long and pretty before, was short and uneven. I didn't recognize her clothes, or the dark winter jacket she was wearing over them.

She stopped walking when she reached me. She smoothed back my hair. My scalp felt like it was waking up from a long time sleeping as her fingers gently touched me.

She was looking at my scar. One thing she could never forget, could never not see.

'Mama,' I said again.

'Baby,' she said, drawing me close. My face got lost in her jacket. It didn't smell like her; it smelled stale and smoky. 'I'm so sorry. I'm sorry.'

I found the gap in the coat and pressed my nose into her sweater. I breathed in more deeply and, underneath, she smelled like Mama, like the lavender soap she always kept in the bathroom. I started crying. She was here, real, finally.

But under the relief there was something else, something dark and hard in the pit of my stomach, in the depth of my chest. My crying was not the crying you do when you know that everything is better now. It was the red, hot bawling of things that still hurt, hurt so much you can't think. So I stopped thinking and it poured out of me, wet and noisy.

Gram prised me away from her. She spoke softly. 'Come, Aubrey, come upstairs.' She pulled me away from my mother, out of the kitchen. Mom sank into a kitchen chair as I left. Her face dropped into her hands in her lap.

'Gram,' I said.

'Honey, I know, I know.' Her arm steered me up the stairs, to my room, and put me to bed.

Gram knocked on my door in the morning. I was already awake, lying on my stomach, one ear pressed into the pillow and one ear up, listening to the quiet in the house.

'Time to get up for school,' Gram said.

'But –' I began.

'She's sleeping,' she broke in. 'And you need to go to school.'

'But – what if –'

'She'll be here when you get back,' she said.

My silence said enough.

'I promise,' Gram said, putting a hand on my shoulder. 'I won't let her go anywhere.'

'How do I know?' I asked.

'Have I let *you* go?'

I shook my head into the pillow.

'That should be enough. Get ready now.'

Gram left me. I got up and dressed.

Ten minutes later she came back to check on me and found me paused outside the closed door to the last extra bedroom at the end of the hallway.

'Come on now,' she said.

Downstairs, she watched me pull on my winter layers and handed me a hot, foiled-wrapped, homemade breakfast sandwich.

'Your lunch is in your backpack,' she said.

I stood numbly in the doorway.

'We're going to talk today, she and I,' Gram said. 'When you get back, it won't be like last night.'

I shrugged. 'Fine. I-I'll be at school, then, if anything . . .'

'It's going to be fine. I'll see you after school,' Gram said, her eyes moving to the window. I looked too, and saw the bus pulling up.

I walked slowly across the lawn.

'Aubrey!' Bridget called. She hurried to catch up with me. I didn't turn or say hi. She stopped next to me. 'What?' she asked.

'My mom's here.'

After the world's longest day of school, the bus finally returned me to Gram's.

The old car, the one that had been Dad's before, was in the driveway.

'Um, bye, Aubrey,' Bridget said. She had walked with me to the car. It was orange and small and beat-up. I put my hand on the trunk. It was dirty and left a film on the fingers of my gloves. 'Does this mean . . . Did she come to get you?'

'I don't know,' I said. 'I just – I mean, we haven't even talked yet.'

I rubbed the fingers of my gloves on my jeans to try to clean them. I swallowed hard.

Bridget walked over to her porch.

I let myself in the house. It was very quiet.

I went first to the kitchen. I put my bag down, took off my heavy coat and boots, and helped myself to a cracker with cheese from a plate Gram had left on the table for me. After I finished chewing, which was hard because my mouth was so dry, I walked up the stairs and to the end of the hallway. Her door was open, and Gram was sitting on the bed with her. They were holding hands, talking softly. I pushed the door the littlest bit. It let out a creak to announce I was there.

They both turned. Gram patted Mom's hand and got up. She walked to the door and nodded to me. 'I'll call you down for dinner and to do your homework,' she whispered. I nodded.

I walked to the bed slowly. Mom was wearing a pair of Gram's pyjamas. They looked funny on her because back home she always slept in big T-shirts. I guess she hadn't packed for this trip.

'What were you and Gram talking about?' I asked.

'Just things, baby,' she said.

Mom looked out of the window. I sat down on the edge of the bed, facing the other way, the doorway.

'Mama?'

'Yeah?'

'How are you?'

She was quiet again, for a long time.

'Sometimes I wonder if life is all about one moment. Everything before and everything after is about that one moment, and we are all stuck there. Do you know what I mean?'

I took a deep breath. 'Yes,' I said.

'I am stuck,' she said.

I flattened my hand on the top quilt, pressing down the

layers of covers. It seemed like my hand would sink forever.

I had been stuck too. I was stuck when I was back at our house, by myself. I was stuck because I couldn't have back what was gone, and I couldn't go forward because I didn't want to start forgetting. But then I had Gram, who made me move forward, even when I didn't want to. And I had Bridget and Marcus, who made me *want* to move forward. My life might have been divided in two because of one moment, but I wasn't stuck any more.

'You can get unstuck, Mom,' I said. 'You can.' I reached for her hand and held it the way Gram had. I pressed each of my fingers, one at a time, into her fingers and waited for her to press back, but Mom's eyes were looking out of the window again.

When I got unstuck, it was without Mom. Maybe her other side of being stuck would be without me too. When I looked down at my hand holding hers, I saw that my knuckles had turned white.

'Lissie,' Gram said, 'I brought your dinner up for you.' She set a tray on Mom's nightstand.

I stretched. I had been sleeping, lying next to Mom on top of the quilt, but I didn't remember falling asleep.

'Come on down, Aubrey,' Gram said.

I went with her without saying anything. Mom waved to me as I left.

When I got to the kitchen, I saw the table looking as it did every night, with our plates, and pots and bowls of food. Tonight there was chicken and green beans and rice and corn bread, and it all smelled wonderful.

'This looks good, Gram,' I said as I sat down.

Gram looked a bit surprised. I usually didn't tell her things like that.

'Thanks, Aubrey,' she said. 'Thank you.'

She piled food onto my plate and passed it to me.

I started eating, but I paused my fork in mid-air over the green beans.

If Mom was back, did that mean this was over now? Would it be back to me taking care of her and myself? Would it mean a lonely, sad house and an empty fridge? What if she took me with her, but she really was stuck forever?

I looked up to see Gram staring at me, so I speared a green bean and started to chew it slowly.

I made it through three periods of the school day before I headed to the little office round the corner from the main office.

'Hi, Aubrey. Everything okay?' Amy asked.

'Yeah – I just – um . . . could I have a snack?'

'Certainly.' She invited me in, and gestured first at the candy jar and then at the chair. 'Sit and stay a while.'

I munched on the M&M's. Amy faced me, showing me I had her attention, even though I wasn't talking.

'Amy?'

'Yeah?'

'Um.' I crunched M&M's shells between my teeth. 'My mom's here.'

I watched Amy's face carefully, but I couldn't tell if the news was a surprise or not.

'Is she with you at your grandmother's?'

'Yes.'

'Tell me about her visit. Did you know she was coming?'

'No. I don't think Gram did, either. She just showed up.'

'Were you happy to see her?'

I looked into the candy jar and picked out just the yellows. One, two, three, four, five, six, seven.

'Amy?'

'Yeah?'

'Do you think this means I have to leave now?'

'Why would you have to leave?'

I scooped up a mixed handful of M&M's and crammed them all into my mouth. When I realized she was still waiting for me to answer, I shrugged.

'Aubrey, I've talked to your grandmother. She's not letting you go anywhere until she's ready, you're ready and your mother is ready. Do you feel like you're ready?'

I took my hand out of the M&M's jar and thought carefully. 'I really want to be with her.'

Amy nodded. 'Can I tell you what I notice about what you've told me?'

I shrugged again.

'It seems that you are worried about having to leave, even if you really want to be with her. It's okay to feel both of those things. It doesn't mean that you don't love your mom if you aren't ready to go, and it doesn't mean that you don't love your grandmother if you do want to.'

I listened. But what if Mom and I both knew that I would never be enough? That I would never make her happy? Would she take me along anyway, and not love me?

'Aubrey?' Amy asked.

Chocolate-sweet saliva ran down the inside of my mouth to my throat.

'Aubrey?'

'I had too much candy,' I said, holding the jar out to her. 'I'm going to be sick.'

'I'm sorry!' Amy jumped up and took the candy jar, then grabbed the trash can and set it in front of my chair. I leaned over it and waited. Amy patted my back.

After a minute nothing had happened, so I slowly sat back up.

When I got home, I headed straight up the stairs. I set my feet solidly on each step, and walked to the end of the hall, to the last door. I pushed it open. She was still there, lying in the bed, sleeping. Her hair was up in a ponytail. The hair tie was a thick purple one that belonged to me. Had Gram given it to her? Had she found it herself?

I set my backpack down, then took off my gloves, hat, winter coat and scarf, piling them on the floor as I stepped out of my boots. I walked to the bed and climbed in next to her, gently waking her up.

'Aubrey,' she said, welcoming me. She was in bed in the middle of the day, but it was not like back home, when she would look at me and not see me. Now she was smiling and wrapping her arms round me. The room felt different too. The window was open a crack, even though it was freezing cold out, so she could breathe in fresh air all the time. 'Tell me about your day,' she said as I nestled into the down comforter she held open for me.

So I told her. I told her about the pop quiz we had in language arts, about how Marcus had sat with us at lunch, about how Bridget had used to love Christian Richards and didn't seem to any more, all of a sudden.

She listened. When I was done talking, she stroked my hair, setting her nose against it, breathing in deeply.

'What?' I asked. 'What are you doing?'

'You smell good,' she said.

'I smell like Gram's soap and shampoo,' I said.

'Well, it smells nice.'

We stayed very still for a long time, feeling each other, warm and present. I liked feeling her against me, and I felt safe like that. But that swish of chocolaty saliva kept coming back into my mouth, like in Amy's office. Eventually I would have to talk, or I would end up stuck again. Maybe stuck forever. I asked an easier question first.

'Why didn't you come on Christmas? You didn't even call.'

'Christmas was just . . . it was too hard.'

'But you're here now. That's not too hard.'

'Christmas is . . . there are just some days of the year that are harder than others. Christmas is probably the hardest day of all. Now, well, these are just regular days. We can start over on regular days.'

It was time for my second question.

'Did . . .' I started to ask. 'Did . . .'

'What, baby?'

'No. Never mind.'

'No, Aubrey, it's okay. Go ahead.'

I took a deep breath, and waited. She waited too.

'Did you love Savannah more than me?'

'Oh no! Aubrey, honey, I'm so sorry. I'm sorry.' I felt her body shake with sobs even though I couldn't hear them. She pressed my hand to her cheek, and I felt that it was wet. 'Of course I didn't. Have you thought that all this time?'

I didn't move. I didn't say anything. I closed my eyes and felt her sadness mixing with mine.

'And how many times I've thought that you should still have your dad instead of me . . .'

I found my voice. It was very small, but it said, 'I never wished that.'

Mom squeezed my hand very tightly. 'I lost them for you. I lost them.'

'It wasn't your fault,' I said. 'It was an accident.'

She didn't say anything for a long time. I whispered again, because I knew, deep down in my heart, that I meant it, 'It wasn't your fault.'

When Gram came up to tell me it was time for dinner, I asked Mom to come downstairs with us. She agreed. So we sat around the table, the three of us, grandmother, mother and daughter, and ate the ham and baked sweet potatoes and baked beans that Gram had made. It was the first time I had sat at a table and eaten with Mom since the last time we ate with Dad and Savannah. I knew she was thinking of it too. Even though it felt heavy in my stomach, the food tasted good and sweet and warm.

Every afternoon I visited with Mom. I showed her my schoolwork, and told her about my friends. I started bringing my homework upstairs and doing it in her bed, or in a chair against the wall. I brought her to my room to meet Sammy. After a few days she was meeting me downstairs when I came home from school. One afternoon Bridget brought over Monopoly for us all to play. One night we watched movies and ate pizza right out of the box in the living room. The next night Mom actually cooked dinner. She made spaghetti and meat sauce. I gave her a kiss on the cheek when she served me.

After she had been with us two weeks, the weather

became unusually warm for January. Mom and I put on our jackets and sat out on the front-porch swing. Martha came out too, and I could tell she was enjoying the breeze and the sunshine.

'Aubrey, I want to talk to you about something.'

'Is it good news or bad news?' I asked.

'It's just news.'

'Okay,' I said.

'I'm going to go back to Virginia in a few days.'

'Oh,' I said, looking away from her.

'Gram and I think that it isn't time for you to come with me yet. I'm going to keep seeing a doctor, and I want to hold a job for a while. I want to work on getting better.'

'You do?'

She nodded. She *was* getting better, I could tell. But one spaghetti dinner wasn't everything.

A few days later it was time to say goodbye. I stood outside the car and hugged Mom for a long, long time. Gram took her turn, and then Mom and I hugged again.

'I'll see you soon, baby,' she said.

'Yeah,' I said. 'Really soon.'

I cried when she drove away. Gram put her arm round my shoulder. 'This is the best thing,' she said.

Soon there was the sound of a door opening, and Bridget crossed her lawn and joined us.

'Hi, Bridge,' I said.

'Hey,' she said. 'Do you want to come over?'

I looked up at Gram, and wiped my eyes on my sleeve. 'Yeah. Is that okay, Gram?'

'It's a good idea,' she said. 'Go on and play.'

Bridget gently caught my elbow with hers, and together we walked back to her house.

19

In February Gram announced that she was going to check on Mom. She was going to go for a whole week.

'Do I get to come this time?' I asked. I'd been talking to Mom on the phone a little. It seemed like she was doing well. She never told me very much; I did most of the talking.

'Not yet, honey. You'll stay with Bridget.'

I might have been annoyed not to get to see Mom, but a week with Bridget sounded really fun. The good thing about February was that we got a whole week off from school. That was new for me, because in Virginia we had our vacation in March. Because Gram picked that week to go, not only did it mean I could have a bunch of sleepovers with Bridget, it meant that we could play together all day too.

On Saturday Gram kissed me goodbye on the porch. 'Be a good girl,' she said. Then she sort of laughed. 'Well, I know you can take care of yourself, but Bridget's mom is expecting you by lunchtime. Take over your things for sleeping. I told her it was okay if you and Bridget want to hang out here for a little bit during the day sometimes, but you two need to sleep at her house. Don't forget about Sammy and Martha.'

'I won't,' I said.

'I love you,' Gram said, giving me a final squeeze.

'Love you too,' I responded. It felt funny to say that out loud.

I liked staying at Bridget's. Her family was fun, and I was comfortable with them. Her dad took part of the week off to spend some time at home too, so it really did feel like vacation.

Over the first weekend Gram called to check in, but it was easy not to think too much about her and Mom when I had Bridget and Mabel to play with. On Monday evening Bridget's dad set up a game of Monopoly that went on from six to ten o'clock, which was when Bridget's mom finally put her foot down and said we'd have to finish in the morning. But Tuesday we woke up and there had been snow in the night, so we went sledding and made snow people in the yard.

Bridget's family had a room in the basement called the

mess room. It could also be called a playroom. There were toys all over it, but, even more fun, there were lots of art supplies and you were allowed to make a mess.

That's what Bridget and I were doing on Wednesday afternoon, making crowns with glitter and feathers all over them, and we had found streamers to hang behind them. We were going to put together costumes too, and put on a play.

'Do you want to play make-up?' Mabel asked. She was crouched on the floor, collecting play make-up into a yellow toy purse. She was having a hard time because she was also holding a pink wand with a glittery star on the end. She was dressed like a fairy, with a gauzy skirt wrapped around her clothes, and pastel wings.

'Not now,' Bridget said. 'But later we will need some make-up for the costumes. You can go practise.'

'Okay,' Mabel said. She climbed up the stairs with her purse.

Our hats were finished in another hour, and we left them to dry and went upstairs to have a snack. Bridget got two pudding cups out of the fridge, and we sat on the couch to eat them.

'Have you seen Mabel?' Bridget's mom asked us.

'Not for a while,' Bridget said.

Her mom disappeared to go look upstairs. She returned in a few moments, leading Mabel by the hand. In her other hand she held an open bottle of orange cough syrup. There was very little left in the bottle.

'How much of this did you drink?' Mabel's mother asked her. It sounded like she had already asked the question but hadn't got a good answer.

'Some,' Mabel said.

'That wasn't a very good idea,' her mother said. 'You know you only take medicine when you are sick, and only what Mommy and Daddy give you.'

Mabel nodded.

'What's the matter?' Bridget asked.

'Mabel got into the cough syrup,' her mother answered. 'Can you find Dad?'

Bridget looked worried, and went to get her father. When he came into the kitchen, he knelt in front of Mabel. 'How do you feel, pumpkin?' he asked.

'Fine,' Mabel said.

'That's good,' he said.

Then Mabel opened her mouth, leaned forward and let out a sticky strand of orange goo into her dad's hands.

'Bridget, Aubrey,' he said, 'get coats, shoes, hats, gloves . . . It's cold outside. Get Mabel's and Danny's too.' Bridget and I understood his not-to-be-questioned tone.

'Where are we going?' Mabel asked.

'To the doctor,' he said.

It was then that Mabel started crying. She wailed as Bridget handed her mother Mabel's little coat and her mother draped it over Mabel's fairy wings.

Within a minute everyone was rushing out of the door, Bridget's mom holding Danny, and her dad carrying a sobbing Mabel. At the last second I grabbed the medicine bottle off the counter and raced outside.

In the car Bridget and I squished between the car seats. Mabel was still crying, but as her dad drove down the hill she opened her mouth again and got sticky orange sick on my jeans.

I caught Bridget's eye. In Bridget's face there was something I had never seen there before. She was scared.

I didn't know how this could have happened. Well, it wouldn't have if Bridget and I had just gone to play make-up with her, like she had asked. We should have been there.

Bridget's dad was driving very fast. Between speeding along the highway and listening to Mabel being sick, I had to cover my own mouth not to be too.

When we got to the hospital, he drove up to the door and let out Mabel and her mother. He parked the car in the lot and hurried us inside, taking the cough-syrup bottle from me to show the doctors. The smell of the hospital hit me, and without a word I ran for the nearest restroom.

I threw up into the toilet and sat down on the floor. I threw up again, and again, and I was still clutching the toilet bowl when I began to remember where I was, and what was going on. *Bridget needs you*, I told myself. *She needs you*.

I stood up on shaky legs. I washed my face at the sink. I rinsed my mouth out and spat, and I took off my hat and pulled my hair back with a little water. I took three deep breaths, then walked to the waiting room.

Bridget was sitting there with Danny, playing with him on her lap. Her parents weren't there.

'Dad said she's going to be fine. They're just checking her out,' Bridget said. 'She's going to be fine, right?'

I looked around and took in the other families in the ER. An old woman by herself, crying. A group of older teenagers, who looked as if they had been skiing because they had boots, goggles and jackets. A pacing man who kept sitting down and jumping right back up again to walk some more.

'You okay?' Bridget asked me.

'Oh. Yeah,' I said, sitting down next to her. Then I remembered. This was her emergency. She was the one who might be upset. 'You? Okay?'

Bridget shrugged. I had no idea what to say.

I wake from a deep, deep sleep. I am not in my room. There is a funny smell and very soft noises made by machines. I feel heavy with blankets and very, very warm, and pretty content to be sleeping.

Someone comes into the room. A woman. She looks soft and nice. She speaks to me softly too. 'It's good to see you're awake, Miss Aubrey.'

My thoughts fluff like cotton balls. I blow at them gently to toss them around like clouds. I don't know this woman. Where are people I do know? Why am I here?

'When we get you off this IV, then we can let you go see your mother.'

Mother. Okay.

What is an IV?

My limbs feel heavy, heavy. I wiggle my fingers and my toes. I feel like stretching my arms, but it would be too hard to get them out from under the blanket.

What about everyone else?

'Where's Dad? Can I go see Dad?'

The woman doesn't say anything. She takes to fixing the blanket around me, tucking it a little tighter.

'Savannah?' I ask. Somewhere under the sleepiness a sharp panic thumps in my chest.

'Sleep now. Don't worry, darling. You just need to go to sleep.'

The car. The bent metal. The glass sparkles. The rain. The blood. The road.

'Where's Savannah?' I yell.

But the soft, gentle woman is too quick. She hurries to the side of the bed, adjusting some of the knobs on the fluid bags there. I can hear her say, 'Deep breaths, deep breaths, that's right.' My eyes grow heavy again, and sleep feels so warm, and nothing is wrong . . .

I heard a small cry. Danny. He whimpered from his spot in Bridget's lap. She was staring into space, as if she didn't see or hear him.

I picked up Danny out of her lap. 'Shhh, shhh,' I said, bouncing him up and down a little. 'Shhh.'

I left Bridget sitting and took Danny for a walk up and down the hallway outside the waiting room. Eventually he stopped crying and put his tired head down on my shoulder and gave in to a nap. He felt so warm and heavy. Would he need to be changed? Maybe someone at the hospital could give me a diaper. I was pretty sure we hadn't packed the baby bag.

There were vending machines in the hallway. In the pocket of my jacket I found a dollar bill and some coins, left over from school snack money. Hugging Danny to my chest with one arm, I pushed the money into the machines and pressed the buttons for a ginger ale and a bag of Cheetos. I collected the food and went back into the waiting room.

'Here.' I held the snack out to Bridget.

She came back from the world she had been staring into. She looked at me and started crying. She stood up and hugged me, getting large, wet tear-tracks all over my shoulder. So I had Danny on one side, and Bridget on the other, and I held them both.

The nurse helps me walk from my bed. I feel a draught on my back and bottom and legs, and realize that my gown is open at the back. I can't make myself seem to care about that, though, and I let the nurse's arm guide me out of the room, down hallways, into elevators.

After a few minutes she brings me to another patient room. I stop in the doorway. There is my mother, in a hospital bed, sitting up, waiting for me.

When I see her there, all alone, that is when I know. I know.

I run to the bed, letting sobs fall out of my mouth and tears run down my face, and she accepts me and presses my face into the blankets at her stomach with her hand in my hair. Her howling is even louder than mine, the loudest pain I have ever heard.

'Hey . . . Bridge . . . Aubrey.'

I felt someone shaking my knee. I opened my eyes to see Bridget's dad kneeling in front of us, his eyes tired but happy. Relieved.

My thoughts jumped with alarm to Danny. I had lost track of him when I fell asleep. But I was still holding him against me, and he was still asleep, just fine.

'She's okay,' Bridget's dad said. 'Everything's fine.'

Bridget started crying again and fell against her dad, who hugged her and chuckled a little at her emotional outburst. 'They just had to clean her tummy out a little more, but they're getting her ready to go home now.' When Bridget kept crying, he held her a little tighter. 'It's all right,' he said. 'She was never in serious danger. Everything's okay.'

Soon Mabel was wheeled through in a tiny wheelchair pushed by a nurse. Her mother walked alongside, sharing Bridget's dad's look of relief. Mabel looked pale but sat like a princess, still in her fairy outfit. She seemed proud of her new bracelet, because she set that wrist across her lap so you could see it. I bet her stomach still hurt, but she seemed to be enjoying the attention. The rest of us joined in the parade. Bridget's mom paused to kiss Danny's head, and then she turned back to Mabel.

I concentrated very hard on holding Danny and making sure I didn't drop him.

Mabel was propped up on the couch with blankets and pillows and *Snow White* to watch. Bridget snuggled next to her. Their dad waited on them, getting them juice and adjusting the TV. Danny stood in his playpen, shouting and holding up toys to show us. Bridget's mom sat on Mabel's other side, twisting Mabel's curls round her fingers.

I didn't feel like hanging out with them in the living room. I walked to the table in the kitchen and sat down by myself, leaving the lights off. I could still hear the movie and Danny.

Eventually Bridget's mom came in to start dinner. She saw me sitting there.

'Aubrey! Why aren't you in the living room, watching the movie with everyone?' She sounded truly concerned.

'I just – this is your family's happy time, you know? You should be together alone.'

She sat at the table next to me, taking both my hands in hers and turning me to look at her. 'You are a part of this family; I want you to know that. I heard you were a great help to Bridget this afternoon, and I couldn't ask for a better friend for her than that. I know it must not have been easy for you to go with us. My girls would love for you to go in there and be with them.'

I nodded. She let go of me, and I went and took my place on the couch.

At bedtime, after pyjamas were on and teeth were brushed, Bridget said, 'Can I sleep with Mabel?'

'What, in her bed?' her dad asked.

'Yeah!' Bridget said.

'No, sweetie, she needs to rest, okay?'

'Fine,' Bridget said. She sounded as if she understood. We went into the girls' room, where an extra mattress had been put on the floor for me. Their mom had already tucked Mabel in and was just finishing reading a story.

'Well, then, Aubrey, sleep up here with me tonight?' Bridget asked.

'That sounds okay,' her mom said. 'Just don't stay up giggling.'

'We won't,' we promised. Her mom turned out the light and shut the door.

Bridget and I climbed into bed. Usually she's the one to hug me or to hold my hand first, but I found myself wrapping my arms round her.

'I was so scared today,' she whispered.

'I know,' I said. 'She's fine, though.' I pressed my face against her chest, a hug.

'You must miss Savannah so much,' she whispered.

'I do,' I whispered back, even more softly. I could hear Bridget's heart beating, and I held on tight.

Dear Savannah,

I used to only be able to think of you one way — since you left, I mean — and that was missing. I hated that you were that — just gone. If I imagined growing up, you were still there, and I had to erase you. Like, if I pictured growing up and coming back to Gram's at Christmas, you were still there, just like all our aunts and uncles always come for Christmas, and my kids played with your kids, just like we always played with our cousins. But my kids won't play with your kids, because you will never have kids, because you will never grow up.

I don't know if you know this, but you should. Mom missed — I mean, Mom misses — you so much. Without you and Dad, she fell apart.

I miss you too. These are the things I miss about you: playing. Waking up before Mom and Dad and making them breakfast. Walking home from the bus stop after school. Sitting around and watching movies in our pyjamas with popcorn. Finding Valentines from you in my schoolbag even though we weren't in the same class and you had to sneak them in secretly. I even miss how Mom made me brush your hair out after showers. Maybe you don't, because I brushed too hard sometimes, on purpose. That was mean. If you came back, I would never do that again.

It's funny, but since I came to live with Gram I think of you differently. You aren't just missing. I have memories of you that seem so real you can't be gone. So maybe, even if I looked for you over the whole world and didn't find you, you have to be somewhere. Are you with Daddy? Are you growing up? Or are you seven forever? Maybe you are somehow older than me now, wherever you are.

To me, you will be seven forever. I'm going to remember you just the way you were. That way I will be able to keep you, sort of, at least a little bit.

You will always be my sister. And I will always miss you. But I also hope that you are happy where you are.

Love,
Aubrey

20

Bridget and I were in her mess room on Sunday afternoon when her dad called from upstairs, 'There's a car outside!'

I looked up at Bridget and realized what her dad meant. 'Gram!' I shouted, abandoning the dry-macaroni palace we were building and scrambling up the stairs.

Gram had stopped the car out front of Bridget's instead of parking in our driveway. She climbed out, and I nearly tackled her in a hug.

She laughed. 'Hi there, duckling. Miss me?'

It wasn't that I'd missed her. I was just glad to see her, now that she was back.

She waved to Bridget's mom and dad, who had come out onto the porch.

'Go get your things. I'm starved. We'll go get something to eat.'

I ran back inside, and Bridget and I tore through the house, collecting my belongings. Somehow I had managed to leave at least one book and a sock in every room. Mabel watched our hurrying with wide eyes.

When I made it back to the porch, Gram was there, thanking Bridget's parents.

'I'm ready,' I said. 'Thank you so much.'

'Thank you, Aubrey,' Bridget's dad said, smoothing my hair, the way he always does with Bridget. 'We had a bit of an emergency this week, and Aubrey knew just what to do.'

'What happened?' Gram asked, looking upset, glancing from one face to another.

'Not to worry. Everything's fine. Aubrey will tell you all about it.' He patted my shoulder. 'You'll come over tomorrow? I think Bridget will miss you.'

I nodded. Bridget's mom kissed my cheek.

I told Gram everything in the car on the way to dinner, but quickly. I wanted to hear things too. 'How's Mom?' I asked.

'Good! I'll tell you more when we get there,' Gram said. 'I'm hungry and I want to pay attention when we talk.' She pulled into the parking lot in front of the diner I'd been to with Uncle David.

When we were seated at a booth, I left my menu shut on the table. I wanted to get right to hearing about Mom, so when the waitress came by, I said, 'I want orange grilled cheese and fries and a pickle and a vanilla milk-shake.'

'Okeydoke,' the waitress said, writing it down. She turned to Gram. 'And for you?'

Gram gave me a playful scowl for rushing her, then shut her menu. 'Tuna on toast.'

'Lettuce, tomato?'

'Yes. And a Sprite to drink.'

When the waitress left, I said, 'Tell me now, please!'

Gram laughed. 'She seems really good.'

'Really?'

'Really.'

'Does she have a job? What's she doing?' Mom had never had a job before. Well, not since I was born, anyway.

'She does. She talked to some of the women at church, and one of them thought it might be a good idea for your mother to work for her. She runs a house for young or ex-pectant mothers who don't have anywhere to go.'

'Why would they not have anywhere to go?'

'Bad luck. Or their families aren't happy about them having a baby.'

'What does she do there?'

'She helps out with paperwork, and some of the clean-ing and cooking.'

Our plates came. I began knocking the slow ketchup out of its glass bottle.

Gram finished chewing a bite of her sandwich. 'She is

getting to directly help people, and I think that is really important right now.'

I twisted a fry in my ketchup puddle.

'Does she spend time with the babies?' I asked.

'I don't think so. I think she works very behind-the-scenes right now.'

We each ate half a sandwich in silence. I slurped at my milkshake. It was tasty, but there was a lot of air in the straw.

'Did she say anything about my birthday?' It was only two weeks away, my birthday. 'Is she coming?'

'I don't think so, honey. She's very excited for you, though – there's a present wrapped in pink paper in the trunk.'

So she was thinking about it. It would be my first birthday without her.

'It's like Christmas,' I said.

'What is?'

'My birthday. She said some days are just too hard. Christmas was too hard, my birthday is too hard.'

'So you understand that she's not coming?' Gram asked.

I took another bite of my sandwich. I loved the butter on the outside. I loved the cheese in the middle that had gone from solid to gooey and back to solid and made my fingers slippery. I loved the dry crust of the bread. Food was either good or it wasn't, usually.

'What would you like to do?' Gram asked.

'Do?'

'For your birthday.'

'Birthday. Right. Oh . . .' I put my sandwich down to think. 'I've never had a pizza party.'

'We can definitely have a pizza party. At the house or out at a pizza place?'

'Um . . . out. And then back to the house for cake and presents.'

'Twelve is quite grown-up, Aubrey.'

'Not really.'

'After twelve is thirteen; is that grown-up?'

'I don't know,' I said. I was a little confused about when you got to be grown-up. Was it the first time you took care of your own mother or lived by yourself or bought your own groceries? I'd already done all those things. 'I don't want to be grown-up.'

'No hurry,' Gram said. 'There certainly is no hurry.'

'Hi, Marcus,' I said as I joined him at lunch on Wednesday. 'Have a good vacation?'

'Disney World,' he said.

'Fun?' I asked.

'I barfed on the plane.'

'Airsick?'

'I ate a whole big bag of cheese puffs.'

'Ew.'

Marcus laughed. 'Where's Bridget?'

'She had some homework to finish. She'll be here in a

minute. Listen. I'm having a birthday party,' I said. 'Do you want to come?'

'When is it?'

'March eleventh.'

'Is that your real birthday?'

'Yes.'

'And you'll be twelve?'

'Yes.'

'I'm already twelve.'

'Okay.'

'Do you like science-experiment kits? I know some great ones where you can grow coloured crystals and then you can smash them.'

'I guess I could like that stuff,' I said.

'Then that's what I'll get you,' he said.

'Does that mean you're coming?' I asked.

Marcus smiled.

21

My eyes opened. It was already a bit light in my room. Everything was quiet. There was a different feeling this morning than on other days.

I am twelve today, I thought.

I stayed comfortably on my side while I thought about that.

I pictured my sixth birthday. The birthday of training wheels and Dad's hand on the back of my bicycle to make me speed along faster.

I remembered my eighth birthday. Savannah and I played with my drooping party balloons. They were soft and floor-bound, then we popped them all by sitting on them, one at a time. Savannah screamed and laughed at every loud bang.

Then there was eleven. Last year. I closed my eyes to linger better in this memory.

'Steak's an awfully grown-up choice for dinner,' Mom says.

'That's all right,' Dad says. 'She can have it. We all can. I'm sure she'll want it with macaroni and cheese.'

'Cheesy potatoes,' I correct him.

Dad smiles at me. He leans in for an Eskimo kiss. When he pulls away, he says, 'Steak and cheesy potatoes, then.'

Had that been my last Eskimo kiss?

'I can't remember, Sammy,' I said out loud. I got out of bed and went to his bowl. He *glupp-glupp-glupped* at me.

Carefully I pressed my nose to the bowl. I stood back up. 'How am I going to do this without them?' I whispered.

There was a knock on the door and I jumped.

Gram opened it. 'Oh good, you're up already. Happy birthday!' She hurried over to hug me. 'We have a busy day! Get dressed quickly. There's a special breakfast for you downstairs. See you in a minute.'

She bustled back out.

Gram's house was never messy, but before the party she seemed to want to give it an extra-good dose of cleaning. She picked me up after school so that I would get home faster than taking the bus, and handed me a list in the car.

1. Hoover
2. Dust
3. Decorate

'What's Hoover?' I asked.

'You know, you get out the Hoover and clean the rugs.'

'What's a Hoover?'

'The vacuum cleaner. All the vacuum cleaners used to be Hoovers.'

Turns out 'hoover' was a verb too, because I 'hoovered' all the downstairs carpets. I found a pink feather duster in the back kitchen closet and then I 'pink-feather-dusted' all the shelves.

After cleaning I got a holidays-only white tablecloth from the linen closet upstairs and put it on the dining-room table. I found the packages of paper party supplies that I'd picked out; they were all purple and silver. I was setting places round the table when Bridget got there.

'Hi!' she said. 'Can I put up the streamers?'

Hanging the streamers turned out to be a two-person job. It involved standing on chairs, trying to twist the strips so that both the purple and the silver showed, and laughing hysterically while getting tangled in the thin crêpe paper. Gram even came in from the kitchen, where she was frosting my cake, to see what was going on. She laughed too, and then decided we could figure it out on our own and went back to the kitchen. Once we had finished, the room looked ready for a real party.

Bridget and I went into the living room and collapsed on the couch, still giggling but exhausted.

There was a knock on the door. I went to open it.

'Hi, Marcus,' I said.

'Happy birthday,' he said, looking embarrassed.

'Come on in.'

'I brought you a present.'

'Thank you,' I said. Was it the science kit he'd told me about? 'I'll put it in the dining room with the others.'

'Okay.' He took one step inside the doorway and stopped.

'It's this way.' I pointed.

'Okay,' Marcus said. He followed me into the dining room.

'Gram!' I called. 'We're ready to go!'

We piled into Gram's car. I sat in the front, and Bridget and Marcus sat in the back. It didn't take long to get to the pizza place. Gram told the waiter to seat us at our own table and to let us order anything we wanted and she would take care of it. She sat at a separate table in the corner with a book.

When we all ordered Sprite, the waiter brought us an extra pitcher of the soda. We began a debate over toppings, but before the waiter could walk away Bridget blurted out, 'Bring us a large pizza with everything on it.'

'Sure thing,' the waiter said, and walked away before any of us could say anything else.

'Everything on it?' I asked. 'What does that mean is actually on it?'

'Everything,' Bridget said. 'That way we don't have to decide, we can just pick stuff off. Everyone gets what they want that way.'

While we waited for the pizza, we plopped drops of water onto our scrunched straw wrappers to turn them into squirmy worms, and when we had done that to all three wrappers, we rolled them into wads and threw them at each other. We started getting really noisy, and I wondered suddenly if Gram would be mad. When I looked up to check, she was smiling to herself while reading her book. There she was, sitting alone with no food in a pizza place, but I don't think she was lonely. She looked happy.

The pizza came.

'Whoa,' Marcus said.

The pizza had piles and piles of, well, everything on top of it.

'Are those meatballs?' Marcus asked.

'All I see are green veggies,' I said.

'Enjoy,' the waiter said, passing out plastic oval plates.

'Thanks,' I said.

We each chose a piece of pizza.

'I don't like peppers and onions,' Bridget said, pulling them off.

I bit the point of my slice. 'Ew. Cooked olives.'

Marcus didn't seem to have a problem with the pizza. He ate his straight, as if it was just a regular piece of pizza. Bridget and I had piles of toppings growing on our plates as we pulled them off.

'Wait, ew,' she said as she spat something onto her plate. 'I think there is anchovy on this.' She sipped her soda and announced, 'I think this was a bad idea.'

'It was *your* idea,' I reminded her, taking a long drink of soda.

We set our slices down, even Marcus.

'You should have let Aubrey pick the pizza,' Marcus said. 'It's her birthday.'

'I don't mind. It was fun to try,' I said. The waiter walked by. 'Excuse me,' I said.

'What can I get you?'

'We need a plain cheese pizza. And take the rest of this one over to my grandmother – she'll like it. She's the lady in the corner with the book.'

'It seems like you guys had a good time,' Gram said after we had got out of the car and were walking towards the house. 'I saw a lot of smiles and heard a lot of laughing.'

'It was fun,' I said, leaning into her arm round my shoulders as we walked. 'What's that on the porch?'

Bridget let out a cheer. She grabbed my arm and pulled me away from Gram as she made me run with her to the porch.

On the porch was a brand-new, shiny, raspberry-coloured bicycle. It had a rainbow ribbon tied to the front vertical bar.

'It has gears and everything,' Bridget said, pointing to the switches on the handlebars. 'And real hand brakes.'

'This is from you?' I asked, amazed.

Bridget nodded. 'And my family. We thought you must

have a bike back in Virginia, but you need one here too. Dad says we can go bike riding on our own this spring, if Gran agrees. Get on.'

I climbed on, but the seat was so high only my toes touched the pedals.

'Dad can fix it,' Bridget said.

Marcus was on the porch now too, admiring the bike.

'I think the phone is ringing!' Gram said. She hurried to unlock the door and disappeared inside. In a few minutes she was back with the phone. 'Aubrey, you have a call.'

I got off the bike. Bridget hopped right on and gave a shriek as it teetered. Marcus handed me the rainbow ribbon. I took the ribbon and the phone into the kitchen.

'Hello?'

'Hi, baby. It's me.'

I sat down in a chair. 'Hi, Mom.'

'Happy birthday.'

'Thanks.'

'Doing anything special?'

'Having a party.' I took deep breaths and my heartbeat slowed to normal. 'How are you?'

'I'm good, Aubrey.'

'Really good?'

'Good.'

I wrapped the rainbow ribbon round my fingers, rolling it tighter and tighter, and then I pulled it off, letting it spiral to the floor.

'Do you still have your job?'

'Yep.'

'What's it like?'

'I just help out at the house, you know.'

'Do you play with the babies?'

'Yeah, sometimes I do. And sometimes I talk to their moms. Or the women who haven't had their babies yet. Some of them are really young and need someone to talk to.'

'You talk to them?'

'Yeah.'

'Do you tell them about me?'

'I do. I tell them all about you. How smart you are. How beautiful you are. How much I miss you.'

'Oh. Is it – is it hard? To see all the babies?'

Mom seemed to think a little. 'It *is* hard,' she admitted. 'I didn't see much of the babies at first. At first, I was just helping out in littler ways, just a couple of hours a day, cleaning and cooking, doing the laundry. Then they asked me to drive some of the girls to their doctors' appointments.'

'And you did?'

'After a few weeks I did, when it really looked like they needed me to. I got to talk to the girls then, you know, on the ride, and sometimes in the waiting rooms at the doctors'. So I talked to them back at the house too. Then I started to come in for more hours, because suddenly there seemed to be so much to do. Some of the girls go out to get jobs, and we need people to watch the babies during the day.'

I felt a lump growing in my throat.

'I've got to get back to my party,' I said. 'My friends are waiting for me. You know, for cake and ice cream.'

'And presents?' Mom asked. I could hear in her voice that she was smiling.

'Yeah, and presents,' I said. 'I didn't open yours yet.'

'Go get it,' she said. 'I can listen to you open it and pretend I'm at your party.'

I carried the phone with me to the dining room, found the pink box and brought it to the kitchen. I sat at the table to open it. It was two books, one with large pictures about life in the Middle Ages, and the other with stiff paper for you to cut out little people and buildings to set up a medieval town.

'You left all your history books here, sweetie,' she explained. 'I thought you might like some new ones.'

'Thank you,' I said. I had almost forgotten about that me, the one who liked to learn things in history books. Mom hadn't.

'Happy birthday. I love you, baby.'

'Bye, Mom,' I said. 'Thanks for calling.'

I hung up before she could say anything else.

Bridget came running in from the dining room. 'Ready, Aubrey? Come on!'

She pulled on my sleeve, and tugged me into the other room.

I forgot all the funny feelings I had on the phone with Mom when I saw the twelve glowing candles on the beautiful cake Gram had made me. It was a chocolate cake but outside it had smooth pure-white icing with pink edges and lettering that said, *Happy. Birthday, Aubrey!* Marcus and Bridget started to sing at the same time.

I was wrong. There were thirteen candles. One to grow on.

Dear Bridget and family,

Thank you so, so, so much for the bicycle. I love it. It was definitely my favourite present this year. I can't wait until it is nice enough out for us to go riding together. I know that Gram knew you were getting it for me because her present was a helmet. She did a good job keeping it secret!

Thank you for being so, so nice to me.

Love,
Aubrey

22

I sat in the living room, surrounded by books for a language arts report on Robert Frost. I had a stack of them in my lap, and I was copying notes out of the top one.

'Hi,' Gram said as she came into the living room.

'Hi,' I said.

She found the remote control on the coffee table and shut the TV off.

'Aubrey, I want to talk to you.'

'Okay,' I said, not looking up from my homework.

'No, I need to know you're really listening,' she said. She pulled the stack of books out of my lap and took the pencil from my hand, and put them on the table. Then she scooped up the poetry anthologies and biographies from the couch cushions, added them to the pile and sat down.

I couldn't tell how serious this conversation was going to be. I couldn't even tell if she was happy or sad.

'I talked to your mother.'

'Oh.'

'We've actually been talking pretty regularly.'

'How often is that?'

'A few times a week.'

'Oh.' I felt like the two of them were being sneaky, with secrets.

'I think she is doing really well, Aubrey.'

'Oh yeah?'

Gram paused for a moment before continuing. 'She wants you to come home.'

I didn't say anything. I didn't know what to say.

'And I think,' Gram continued, 'if you wanted to, it would be okay.'

'Are you sending me back?'

'I said if you wanted to. You can stay here as long as you like, you know that. But I think this is what you've both been working towards, isn't it? And if you are ready, and she is ready, then you can go if you like. I wouldn't just send you off, either. I'd come down and stay with you for a while. And once the two of you were on your own there would be a social worker to check in and make sure things were okay too.'

Over months and months Gram had never let me decide anything. She made me move to Vermont. She made me get out of bed. She made me go to school. She tried to control when I got to see or talk to Mom. And now she was going to let me make this big decision?

'Well, what do you think?' I asked. Maybe she could make this one for me too.

Gram thought for a few minutes. 'I would miss you a lot, duckling. But, I think, you can look into your heart and figure out what you want.'

My heart was a confused place. All that night it jumped with excitement and intense happiness. I dreamed of Mom, and us together again. I dreamed it both when I was asleep and when I was lying awake. I missed her so much, and there she was, within reach.

The other half of my heart was heavy and dark. It made me think things I didn't want to. It felt like being hungry, or scared, or lonely. I didn't know why my heart would have those things inside it too, when I should have been happy.

It is hard to hug a fish. But I tried. I carefully took Sammy's bowl and sat on my bed, holding my arms round the bowl. I think he was confused. He fluttered his fins quickly. Maybe my arms round him made it seem darker than he was used to.

'I'm sorry, Samkins,' I said. I thought about Sammy. 'You've been with me a long time, haven't you?'

How long did betta fish live?

Pet fish don't always hang around very long. Sammy had been good to me, living through the whole summer and fall and winter. A fish could die any day. Sammy could die any day.

'Don't leave me, Sammy,' I whispered.

But, really, anybody could die any day, whether you were ready or not. It could be your pet fish or your sister or you. Nothing is the same forever.

'Where will you be then, Sam?'

Did I need to hurry and get to Mom because you never know how much time there is? Or did it not matter, because we'll all be together again, some day, anyway?

'Bridget?'

'Yeah?'

'I have to tell you something.'

Bridget stopped spinning her swing. She had been twisting the ropes for a big push off, but she untwisted them and the swing hung straight. 'What?'

'My mom called. She didn't talk to me; she told this to Gram to tell me. She wants me to come home.'

'Oh,' Bridget said in a very small voice. 'You have to go, right?'

'No. Gram said I could choose.'

'But you want to go.'

'I don't know.'

Bridget turned to look at me. 'You don't know if you want to be with your mom?'

'I mean, of course I do. I really, really do. All I've been wanting all year is for things to be right again.'

Bridget looked hurt for a moment, then looked back down at her tennis shoe, whose tip she circled in the dirt.

'I'm sorry,' I said. 'I mean, I love being here with you too.'

'Maybe your mom could come up here. You could both live with Gram.' Bridget sounded like her idea was the perfect solution.

'Gram says that she and Mom talked about it, and Mom doesn't want to have to be taken care of by another adult. She wants to have her own life.' I had to think about how to explain it. 'It might be like, if Mom came to live with Gram, she would never be making things better, but staying in the same place.'

'I don't get it,' said Bridget.

'I don't really get it, either.'

Bridget shrugged.

'What's the matter?' I asked.

'I don't want you to go away.'

'We can still be friends. I would come back to Gram's, of course.'

'Not friends like now. Not like next-door, everyday kind of friends.'

'You have other friends.'

'Not the same.'

'Bridget, I'm sorry.' Bridget always tried so hard to listen, to understand. But now it seemed like she was thinking about what *she* wanted. 'I might need to go home.'

She sat quietly, but only for another minute or so before she got up, slid off her swing and said, 'See you tomorrow.'

I sat on the swing in her yard, wishing that our conversation had gone differently. Maybe I shouldn't have told her at all.

~~Dear Mama,~~
    ~~You think we are ready, but how do you~~
~~know?~~

23

Bridget and I sat on the bus in silence on the way to school, and then through lunch with a rather confused Marcus trying to make conversation between us, and then again on the bus home. After I told Gram I was home and dropped off my backpack, I walked to Bridget's and her mom let me in. I found Bridget in her room, furiously cutting cardboard cereal boxes into shapes and then gluing them together into structures.

'What are you making?'

'A town,' she answered.

'Can I help?'

Bridget looked at me with raised eyebrows, then shrugged. I got some scissors and found a whole box and just sat there with both in my hands, not sure what to make.

'I think I might stay here,' I announced. It was hard to say that out loud. It made it feel like the truth, like I had decided, even though I hadn't, not yet.

To my surprise Bridget started to cry.

'It was what I said, wasn't it?' she asked. 'Now you're not going to go be with your mom because of me. She's going to be all alone and it is my fault, because we had a fight.'

'What?' I asked.

'No, you have to go,' she said, crying harder.

'Why?'

'Because kids are supposed to be with their moms, if they can,' she sobbed. 'I told my mom everything, and that's what she told me, that you and your mom should be together if you can, so go!'

I had never seen Bridget look so upset – angry, and confused – and she was almost turning purple she was crying so hard.

I didn't know what to do. She turned away from me, to the wall. When she didn't turn back, I let myself out of her room, and left her house.

'Have a seat, Aubrey. How is everything?'

'Fine.' I slouched into the chair in Amy's office.

'Just fine?'

'Just fine.'

'I hear you have a big decision to make.'

'So you talked to Gram?'

'She thought I should know.'

Amy let a pause hang in the conversation. I figured I was supposed to fill it.

'I don't know what to do,' I said.

'Have you and your mother talked about it?'

'No.'

'It might help. That way you could both be clear about what you expect to happen.'

I shook my head. 'I can't talk to her.'

'Why not?'

'If I heard her voice, and she asked me, I would say yes right away. I wouldn't think about it. I would just say yes.'

'So you can think of a reason not to say yes?'

'Yes – no – I mean, sorry. I got confused.'

Amy smiled. 'That's okay. It seems to me you are doing really well here. And if you wanted to stay here, because you feel safe at your grandmother's, or because you are happy with your friends here, or because you like school, that would be a good choice. On the other hand, it would also be a good choice to live with your mother again, because I know it has been really hard for you to be apart. You don't have to decide right away, and your decision doesn't have to be permanent.'

I hadn't thought of that. Something about that idea seemed funny, though.

'I don't know. I don't want to just sit here and not decide, because then I'll think about it every day, whether I should just make a choice. And it would be so hard – to go there – and to find out – it was a mistake. I need to be sure.'

'So you have decided to make a decision. That's good. That in itself is really positive.'

'I'm back where I started.'

'Of course you aren't. You may be in one of many places, but none of them is where you started.'

When I didn't take my turn to talk, Amy started talking again.

'Well, it seems we have come to a stopping point for today. My door is open to you, though, if you want to come back again. You have a lot to think about, and I'm here.'

'Thanks,' I mumbled. I held out my hand.

Amy shook it, and laughed. 'How formal! Even if you decide to go, this isn't goodbye. We'll certainly talk again before you leave.'

I nodded. It felt weird to say bye, even if it was just for now, so I didn't say anything. Only when I was out in the hall did I realize I hadn't even thought about M&M's once while I was in there.

'Where's Bridget?' Marcus asked when he found me sitting alone at lunch.

'We're . . . we're not talking today.'

Marcus sat down across from me. 'Again? You guys don't not talk. You always talk.'

'I know,' I said. 'But not today.'

Marcus shrugged. He started to eat his hamburger. I picked up my can of soda to take a sip, then put it down and started playing with the tab.

'I have to tell you something,' I said. 'Um . . . my mom is doing okay . . . and she wants me to come home. I don't know if I want to go yet, but I'm thinking about it.'

Marcus stopped chewing his hamburger. 'Do you need an ice-cream bar?' he asked. 'I think I need an ice-cream bar.' He reached into the pockets of his baggy corduroys and fished out some change. He sifted through it and then hopped up. He came back from the lunch line a few minutes later with two ice-cream bars.

The ice-cream bars sat on the table, getting melty, as he continued to eat his hamburger, and as I continued to pull at the tab instead of drinking my soda.

'I'm sorry,' I said. 'I didn't know how to tell you, because I knew it would make you upset, hearing about my mom when . . .'

'What?' Marcus asked. 'I'm not upset about that.'

'What's the matter, then?' I asked.

'It's just that . . . I would miss you,' Marcus said. He looked at me while he said it, even though he never looks straight at people when he talks to them.

Even though I was surprised, I knew I meant it when I said, 'I would miss you too.'

The doorbell rang. I got off the couch to answer it.

It was Bridget. I didn't remember her ever ringing the doorbell before.

'Hi,' she said.

'Hi.'

She held up a covered plate. She handed it to me, and I peeked under the foil.

'Cookies,' she said. 'Chocolate chip. Mom and I just made them. I should have invited you to help . . . but . . . next time.'

'Next time,' I agreed. 'Come in.'

She followed me to the couch. She took off her tennis shoes and sat down next to me with her feet under her. I peeled back the foil and took a cookie. It was still warm, and the chocolate was melty. It was baked just enough so that it was still really soft, just the way the best cookies are. Nothing had ever tasted better.

Bridget watched me eat for a minute.

'Aubrey?'

'Yeah?'

'You're my best friend.'

'I know,' I said. 'You're mine too.'

Bridget was quiet for another minute. 'You don't know yet, do you?'

I shook my head.

I set the plate on the coffee table and we sat, still and quiet, for a few minutes.

'Bridget?'

'Yeah?'

'Can I tell you something?'

'Yeah.'

'I really want to go home.'

Bridget waited, leaving her eyes on me.

'Sometimes I imagine going back to Virginia. I ride down on the train by myself.'

'Why the train?'

'Because that's how I got here.'

'Would they really make you go by yourself?'

'No, Gram said she would come. But when I imagine it, I'm by myself. And when the train stops at the station, I get off, and I stand there. And I look down the platform one way. And then I look the other way. For my mom . . . And there is no one there.'

'That's not going to happen,' Bridget said.

I looked down and spoke in a very small voice. 'I know. Or, at least, I'm trying to tell myself that. But when I imagine it that's what I see.'

'Aubrey, it's going to be okay. Everything is going to be okay.' Bridget moved closer to me on the couch. She wrapped her arms round me and hugged. She hugged me for a long time. After a while she got up. I stood up too, while she put on her shoes, and we walked to the door.

'Don't forget you're my best friend,' she said.

'I won't,' I promised. I held up my hand, offering her my flat palm. She pressed hers to it.

When we lowered our hands, she said, 'Bye, Aubrey.'

'Goodbye.' After Bridget had walked off the porch without looking back, I shut the door.

Home

24

Gram seemed to be giving me plenty of time to think, so I was surprised when late one afternoon she came into my room.

'You got some mail,' she said.

'Really?' I asked, not moving from my bed. 'Who's it from?'

'Your mother.' She set two envelopes gently on my bed. I didn't look at them, just at her. I sat up a little and reached for her before she moved away. I hugged her.

'I love you, Gram.'

Gram chuckled. 'I love you too, you silly girl. Now open that stuff up and see what it says.' She left the room, closing the door, and I scooped up the envelopes.

The larger one looked like it had been opened once before and then taped shut again. I opened it first.

Four faces looked up at me. Though they were extremely familiar, they also seemed to be from some other time and place. It was us: me, Savannah, Mom and Dad. It was the picture I had taken from Mom's room and left on the counter in Virginia.

I set it down to rip open the other letter. My mother had written it, on loose-leaf.

My dear Aubrey,

Not long ago I discovered and opened up a mysterious unaddressed envelope. Then I knew where the picture from the frame on my dresser had disappeared to. I thought for only a minute before I realized that you must have wanted it. Even if that guess was wrong, I want you to have it.

I want you to know that I am doing well here. I have put fresh paint in the living room and dining room. They are both now a sunny yellow. They look quite different than before, I have to say. I have cleaned up your room but I won't paint it quite yet - I want you to choose your own colour.

I like my job better all the time. It feels good to be helping people, and

the babies are, of course, delightful.
I have full-time hours now, which
means I am working a lot, but as soon
as you return, they will let me go back
to part-time for as long as I need to,
so that we can spend some time
together.

Know that I am thinking of you, for
all of every day.

Love,
Mama

I read her letter three times. Then I set it aside. I picked up the photograph again and took it over to my desk, closer to the window, to look at it in better light.

There we all were, frozen in that one moment, so happy. I had thought we were gone forever, but it wasn't true. My family would never come back to me, but I did have little things, little reminders. This picture. And Mom still there, and getting better. And my memories.

Holding the picture in front of me, I closed my eyes. I could still see it. I could feel the memories right there, close, but they weren't drawing me inside like they sometimes did. Maybe it was up to me now. I thought about Mom and whether I should go to her, and about Dad and Savannah, and then I chose the memory I wanted, and waited for it to fill me.

* * *

I've been sick for three days.

Mom says it's one of those spring flus. She says some people get sick when the seasons change. Maybe I'm one of those people, maybe not. All I know is it's Wednesday and I haven't been to school yet this week. I'm sick of spending all day on the couch, but my pillow still feels good and the sheets are smooth and cool and standing makes me dizzy.

Mom sits me up, makes me drink water out of a baby cup we still have for some reason. It only turns up when we don't feel good. The sick cup.

'Mama . . .'

'Yes, baby?'

'I don't feel good.'

'You're sweating. Do you know what that means?'

I did. Dad always talks about that, that a fever happens and your body gets really hot. When you start sweating, it means the fever is gone.

'Get up, come in the car to get Savannah.'

I shake my head.

Mom pushes the hair back off my forehead. She pauses for a minute, holding my hair that way.

'Okay. You're not ready. Lie back down. I'll be back in fifteen minutes.

When I next open my eyes, Savannah is there, watching TV. She wears a pink plaid jumper over a green shirt. Her sneakers are her baby-blue high-tops with rainbows and clouds.

'Did you dress yourself?' I ask.

'Mama let me,' she says, not turning round.

Mom comes back into the living room and announces, 'You're going outside.'

'See ya, Savannah.'

'You too,' Mom says to me. 'The air will help you.'

She stands me up, and I change into the clean clothes she has brought me, even my underwear, right there in the living room. Then she pushes me and Savannah, who has an armload of toys, out into the front yard.

'Let's play house,' Savannah suggests. I sit down on the grass, determined not to move an inch.

Savannah opens her little portable dollhouse and starts handing me the tiny people from inside: A pale wooden boy with fuzzy yellow yarn hair. A brown wooden boy with black hair. A lanky, bendy-plastic ballerina.

'Those are the brothers and the sister,' she explains. She holds up a squat plastic woman and a tall wooden man with red string hair. Then she shows me a wine cork with a face drawn on it. 'Mama, Daddy, baby.'

'Savannah, none of these people go together. They aren't a family.'

Savannah doesn't seem to care. 'They live in the same place.'

'That doesn't matter.'

'And they are happy together. So there.'

Too tired to argue, I set the children in their beds. I put my elbow on my crossed legs and rest my head on my hand.

Dad's car pulls into the driveway. I don't get up, but Savannah runs to meet him. They walk to where I'm sitting.

'How's my girl?' Dad asks. 'What are you up to?'

'Playing house. But Savannah made up a crazy family.'

'Ah, that happens. But I'm sure it's very nice, right?'

I shrug.

'Are you feeling better?'

'Maybe,' I say.

'Maybe,' he echoes. 'Well, that's better than not at all. It's better than not at all.'

Though I am nine, and way too big for it, Dad picks me up, letting my head rest on his shoulder.

'You'll be fine, girl,' he says.

'I love you, Daddy,' I say.

'I love you too.'

'And me?' Savannah cries from below, where she holds his hand. 'Do you love me?'

'And you, Savannah,' he says. Savannah squeals happily and hugs his arm. 'I love both my girls. Savannah, get your toys.'

She scoops the dolls into the house, shuts it and takes his hand again.

Savannah leads us up the steps and pushes open the un-latched door, not letting Dad go. I am content in his arms. He carries me inside and nestles me back into my cocoon on the couch. Savannah sets the dollhouse next to me.

Mom calls them to dinner and they leave me, but I hear them talking, eating, laughing together. Alone on the couch, I open the dollhouse and look through Savannah's little people, pausing carefully to look at each face, wondering if they could be, as Dad has said, a family that is still very nice.

When I lifted my head up from my desk, I wiped away

the tears that had run all over my face. There weren't more behind them. I was done crying.

As I wiped the wet spot off my desk, my palm made a slight squeak. I rubbed the spot with the sleeve of my sweatshirt to make sure it was gone.

I took the photograph and held it in my hands. I smiled at each of them, Savannah, Dad, Mom. Then I set it to lean against the wall, so I could look at it while I wrote.

Dear Mama,

I know that you are ready for me to come home. I am really happy that you want me to.

But I am not ready yet.

I am happy here with Gram. She is really good to me, even when I am being a baby. I love school, and I have good friends. I really want to finish the year, at least. The family next door is really nice to me. My best friend lives there.

Now, here is like home.

I miss you. I know that you miss me, and that you love me, and that you want me to be with you. I promise that I will come home to you, some day, but I am not ready yet. I know that you want us to be a family again. I want that too. I'm just not ready to leave the family that I have here. Please come visit again. I hope that everything is good, and your new job is still good, and you are getting ready for when I do come back to Virginia.

Everything is going to be okay.

Love,
Aubrey

ACKNOWLEDGEMENTS

Thank you to my wonderful agent, Elizabeth, and the team at Curtis Brown. Your faith in me, as well as your careful attention, never ceases to amaze me. I feel so blessed to have you watching over me.

Thank you to my editor, Wendy, as well as Caroline Meckler and the whole team at Random House. You offered the perfect balance between detailed suggestions and creative space, and I am extremely grateful.

Thank you to my professors at the New School: Tor Seidler, Sarah Weeks and Susan Van Metre, who provided extensive critiques of this piece from its very beginning; and David Levithan, who kept me inspired with the best of children's literature and his unceasing, invaluable support. Thank you also to the members of my MFA Writing for Children class, who lent their support, provided crackers and cheese, and critiqued this piece both in class and out with honesty and generosity: Kate Gilliam, Jeff Imrich, Chee Wan Kim, Caron Levis, Paula McAlister, Eric Moffat, Stefanie Pivar, Cait Stuff and, especially, my Favourite and my Anemone, Anne Heltzel. You helped shape Aubrey and me.

Thank you to Katherine Ehrlich, who shared her knowledge of psychology in the form of advice not only for plot and characters, but also for emotional support while I wrote this story. You were always ready to talk when I needed you.

Thank you to my kids at the Anderson School. You probably didn't realize it, but it was your presence in my life and your insatiable love for books that kept me writing. Some of you were the first kids to hear this story, and your comments were invaluable. I wish I could list you each by name, but as there are over a hundred of you, you know who you are: Ms Puzo's classes of 2006–07 and 2007–08, 3-228 and 3-238, and my ELA crew of 2007–08, 5A and 5B.

Thank you to my first reader, Erika 'Ms Puzo' Vaughan, who read faithfully without criticism, listened continuously without interruption, hugged readily without request and believed in me endlessly without question. You shared your classroom, not to mention all those grapefruit and strawberries; I could not ask for a better environment in which to write a book, nor a better friend to share it with. Thank you for holding my hand.

Finally, thank you to my parents, who raised me with love, laughter and libraries, and to my siblings, who taught me everything else important, like how to transport fish on trains.

It all started with a Scarecrow

Puffin is well over sixty years old.
Sounds ancient, doesn't it? But Puffin has never been
so lively. We're always on the lookout for the next big
idea, which is how it began all those years ago.

Penguin Books was a big idea from the mind of
a man called Allen Lane, who in 1935 invented
the quality paperback and changed the world.
**And from great Penguins, great Puffins grew,
changing the face of children's books forever.**

The first four Puffin Picture Books were hatched in 1940 and the
first Puffin story book featured a man with broomstick arms called
Worzel Gummidge. In 1967 Kaye Webb, Puffin Editor, started the
Puffin Club, promising to **'make children into readers'**.
She kept that promise and over 200,000 children became
devoted Puffineers through their quarterly instalments of
Puffin Post, which is now back for a new generation.

Many years from now, we hope you'll look back and
remember Puffin with a smile. **No matter what your age
or what you're into, there's a Puffin for everyone.**
The possibilities are endless, but one thing is for sure:
whether it's a picture book or a paperback, a sticker book
or a hardback, **if it's got that little Puffin
on it – it's bound to be good.**